I0732133

Published by:
Powder River Publishing LLC
1014 Black Mountain Road
Thermopolis, Wyoming 82443

Copyright © 2023
ISBN:
Printed in the United States of America

No part of this publication may be reproduced, stored, transmitted in any form — electronic, mechanical, digital photocopy, recording, or other without the express written approval of the author.

All rights reserved solely by the author. The author guarantees all are original and do not infringe upon the legal right of any other person or work. The views expressed in this book are not necessarily that of the publisher.

All photography was used with the permission of the photographers and cannot be used, or reproduced without the express written permission of the photographer.

Table of contents

"And they said to him, 'Inquire of God, please, that we might know whether the journey on which we are setting out will succeed.'"

Judges 18:5

"Gone, glimmering through the dreams of things that were."

Lord Byron

"Come, my coach! Good-night ladies; good night, sweet ladies; good night."

Ophelia, from "Hamlet"
William Shakespeare

Once I graduated from my rehab stint in the late summer of 2002, I was of the mind that maybe I needed to try something different with the next phase of my life, else the chances were fairly good I was going to end up back behind the manicured fences of the Hannah Hills Rehabilitation Center again, sooner this time rather than later.

My father must have been thinking along the same lines, because on the morning he and my mother picked me up in his Buick to take me home from Hannah Hills he'd already mapped out some plans for the future on my behalf.

"After we have lunch and you get settled in," he told me in his decidedly no-nonsense-anymore manner, "I want you to ride out to your Uncle John's shop and have a little sit-down with him. He might have an opportunity for you there."

He didn't offer me more of an explanation than that, but I had the feeling things had already been decided for me while I'd been away doing my time getting straight so I could rejoin polite society again. Probably my father—and I can't blame him much for this—was of the opinion that I needed a push in the right direction these days, even if I was twenty-seven and had a sheepskin from the University of Tennessee in Knoxville in my possession, because it was certainly true that in the five years since graduation I hadn't taken up much impetus for traveling on the straight and narrow on my own. I'd gotten sacked from my job selling electronics at a big box store because I'd allowed a few sundry items to go out the front door and off the receiving dock in exchange for some quick cash to support my burgeoning romance with recreational drugs. It was a good thing I was well-liked and had no enemies at the store, because prosecution for theft was dropped in exchange for my voluntary resignation, a promise to pay back the two thousand bucks I'd mishandled, and to enroll in a drug treatment program at Hannah Hills, a stay which was to take up the next six weeks of my life. If I lived up to those terms, my record would be expunged and I wouldn't have to go around the rest of my life like some half-assed Charlie Mansion with a criminal background.

So, after stumbling through the unhappy circumstances that had shaped my destiny and curtailed the majority of my far-fetched dreams, I now found myself at a philosophical standstill. Life can rap you across the knuckles and tell you what a bad boy you'd been and how you ought to be ashamed of yourself for all your trespasses, but after a while you get a little tired of hearing about it. When my father dispatched me out to my uncle's place of business to help me get back on the road to hard work and respectability, I arrived there with my outward self holding my hat contritely in my hands, but also carrying within my inner self a determination to somehow discover a new path to a land full of treasures and divulgences that would shelter me from life's upcoming storms and bring me pleasure for the rest of my life, until the day I died an old man with a smile on my face or until somebody blew my brains out just for the hell of it, which is the way things seem to go a lot in the world these days. I wasn't sure if I wanted to be a villain or a man of esteem about town; all I really knew was there had to be some way to elevate my being from the worn playgrounds and abandoned ruins of my sorry past, there had to be a way to discover a passageway to a place where I didn't have to laugh to keep from hurting or have to recount with pain and remorse what was lost and spent, that maybe there was a repose where I could instead live in anticipation of the dreams that were to perhaps come my way in the sweet bye and bye. No, I cared very little about any job that might steer me back onto the proper path for a young man to take; it was all about what wonder might befall me in new surroundings that mattered the most to me, what whispers of romance and magic that might be found in the golden sunsets and secret nights I'd visited once or twice before in my limited life and not once had ever tired of, and how with a fair amount of effort and luck I might come to abide in such a place permanently.

I grew up on the east side of Nashville, the working-class area, and attended public schools there all the way up to graduation, when I left the city for four years to party down at the University of

Tennessee in Knoxville. I hadn't been much of an athlete during my high school days, so I didn't go to Knoxville to star on the football team or anything like that, but I did manage to participate in a lot of drinking and getting rowdy on game days, performing at those tasks so expertly that I came close to flunking out toward the end of my sophomore year and had to shift gears and become a real-life student just to stay enrolled. So, as it was, it wasn't like any elite corporations were beating the bushes to secure my services when my school days came to an end. I'd worked Christmas holidays and summer vacations in the past at a big electronics store selling audio systems and stereo components and big screen televisions, so it was fairly simple to go with them fulltime and stay where I could maintain the status quo. But after a while I went drug crazy and everything fell apart and I got sent to Hannah Hills for a spell. It was a pretty crappy place to have to hang out in but it certainly beat the crap out of prison.

But now that I was free to roam the streets again, I felt like there were a million routes to travel but not a single one I could set forth on without some dire consequence awaiting me on the horizon. I felt like any choice or decision I made I'd only screw it up in the end as I'd managed to do my entire life so far, so this time I mentally threw up my hands and decided to take an oh-well attitude and wait to see where the winds of fortune would take me. When dear old Dad dispatched me to my uncle for possible employment, I told my feet to take me there without tripping and stumbling and when I arrived to take a good gander at what possibly could lay in store for me if I decided to take on a new profession.

My Uncle John, my father's older brother, was the only well-off member of our middle-class family, the only one of four siblings to own a business and not be employed by someone else, mainly because as the oldest son of the family he'd been assigned the job of executor of his parents' estate and had used that position to appropriate most of the wealth my grandparents had managed to muster, and with the promise of furthering the family fortunes in the future by virtue of investments, he'd bought into several small business ventures and at the same time started a foreign car repair shop that prospered and became well-known, so much that wealthy automobile owners from all over soon came to be dying to throw all their money at getting their cars serviced there. The company became highly regarded throughout the South as absolute experts at the repair and restoration of foreign cars, all this despite the fact my uncle was not any kind of mechanic at all. What he didn't know about the intricacies of an expensive foreign car, however, he made up for by investing and hiring the best servicemen and mechanics around and built the company up to a highly revered business. If some tycoon had a Jaguar that needed tending to, he brought it to Wright's Foreign Car Repair to get fixed correctly. Reservations were made weeks and months in advance. The price was astronomical but never discussed or haggled over, for this was not a hobby where money played much of a factor. This was a rich man's game, and money was only a small part of it.

Back in the days when I was an upcoming high school senior, as an early graduation gift Uncle John had surprised me with a 1972 MG Midget, then some twenty years old but fully restored. I'd only owned one car before then, a sad Ford Pinto that was pretty well dilapidated when I'd bought it the summer after my sixteenth birthday and then had to sell six months afterward for junk when the engine blew. I'd been a pedestrian and a bummer of rides for some time when the Midget came into my possession, and although it was fairly old it was nonetheless fire-engine red and a convertible and a four-speed, and no one else in school had anything quite like it, so it was special in that way. For my entire senior year, the Midget was a chick magnet, and I loved it dearly for that and loved my uncle for bestowing such a gift to me, because I needed all the help I could get in that particular department.

But a woman ran into the back of the Midget at a four-way stop my sophomore year in Knoxville, and the car was never the same again. I took it back to Uncle John's shop for repair, but three weeks later he called and pronounced it dead from acute frame damage. He said if I wanted, he could find another two-seater for me, but I didn't want to wait and be patient and so took the insurance money from the wreck and bought a soulless Honda Civic to cart me around, a sad thing that did nothing to enhance my social life. I was still driving it eight years later, punching the buttons on the radio on that Friday afternoon as I drove to my uncle's shop to discuss my prospects for the future with him.

Uncle John's place of business was no hole in the wall with junk parts and discarded automobiles scattered about like most garages you see. To the contrary, Wright's Foreign Car Repair looked more like a clean and livable small town from Currier and Ives, with a cozy and spacious office area and a supply room as large as a meeting lodge at a ski resort and a waiting room suitable for reposing for a lengthy spell if one was of the mind to, with vending machines and strategically-placed televisions and current magazines and free coffee, comfortable chairs and strong wi-fi for those with business or social networking to attend to. Waiting at Wright's, however, was not truly a feasible thing for my uncle's clientele, since a shiny minivan waited outside the door to carry customers to work or home or wherever they wished and then return to pick them up later in the day when their vehicles were ready to go.

The service garage consisted of numerous stalls, all equipped with state-of-the-art tools and diagnostic machines, manned by neat, freshly-laundered men in grey work uniforms with their names stitched in red across their shirt pockets. There was never a sign of grease or motor oil anywhere to be found, a fact which always puzzled me because it was hard to see how automobile maintenance could be accomplished without the presence of smudge, but nothing but clean surfaces was ever present at Uncle John's. In the back of the garage was a separate area for body work and paint, and one fellow—the only black man on the premises—worked eight hours each day detailing and cleaning to the ultimate tee the numerous sedans and coupes and roadsters brought in by appointment, delivering them back to their owners shining and showroom new.

"Frank back there," Uncle John pointed out to me that afternoon, "has been detailing cars for us going on thirty years now. He's close to being a rich man these days, but he had nothing when I hired him. He does a hell of a good job, so I make certain he's always taken care of. Whatever Frank needs, Frank gets."

We were sitting in Uncle John's office, which had a glass window on one wall where he could look out into the service area and see if everything was humming along in an efficient manner. I could see he was still a hands-on boss after all these years. He had everything going the way he liked. He pulled up a job requirement form from his computer, printed it off, and handed it to me across the desk.

"Think you can live up to these commandments?" he asked with a smile. Yeah, he was smiling, but I knew he was serious underneath his grin. Uncle John didn't hire anybody at his shop unless they were pretty much exceptional, so I knew he was lowering his standards and throwing me a bone because I was his nephew and his little brother's kid, but I also knew he wouldn't put up with having a first-class fuckup around for too very long, even if I did happen to be family.

I looked over the paper to see if I should just get up and split that very minute, knowing the possibility existed I'd never be able to live up to what I signed my name to, but I knew if I didn't sign on the dotted line that later I'd be kicking myself in the butt for not giving myself the opportunity to escape the disastrous quagmire I'd allowed myself to sink into in the past few months. This, I told myself, may end up being the only means of escape I'll ever have to change the direction of my existence. Better not blow it, bubba.

There were rules about appearance and punctuality, dependability and honesty, stuff that almost reminded me of the Boy Scout Credo. Basically, the page read like it was a guideline on how to be a valuable enough employee at Wright's so as not to get sacked right from the get-go. The one that really caught my eye was the edict about having good moral character. My uncle's employees weren't allowed to rob banks, drive drunk, or take drugs any stronger than Tylenol. I wondered again if I was prepared to reform myself from any or all of my wicked days and nights of the recent past just to get this job.

I agreed to the regulations though, and soon found myself herded out of the office to meet with Doris, a fiftyish-looking old bag who handled all the billing and appointments and comings and goings for Wright's. She proceeded to make copies of my W-2 and Social Security card and had me fill out an employee information form on a touch screen tablet, and afterwards, with a card in my possession, I was sent to a walk-in clinic down the road for a mandatory drug test, a procedure which would have signaled curtains for me two months prior, but now, because of my sojourn at Hannah

Hills, was a piece of cake, since all traces of my former drug-riddled life was now a clean slate, like Jesus Christ Himself had come in and made all my sins disappear.

I was to report to work on Monday of the following week. Eight o'clock sharp, Doris instructed me like an elementary school librarian. She would have a uniform ready for me then.

It occurred to me on the way home that I had no earthly idea what my job duties were. I knew a little about foreign cars because of my past MG Midget ownership, but it was scant knowledge for such a place as Wright's Foreign Car Repair. In all probability, I'd have to stumble and bullshit my way through each day and situation, but in a sense this revelation relaxed me, since it seemed not at all different from the way I'd lived my life up until then.

• • • •

Like I figured, I wasn't entrusted with much responsibility my first few weeks on the job. I was assigned to Uncle John's top mechanics that first week, shadowing them from task to task and going from one to the other, standing by while they tended to automotive problems and offered advice and solutions for the perplexing problems for the more recalcitrant models in for repair, some of these cars so exotic and rare I had no idea they even existed. There were Ferraris and Jaguars and obscure Triumphs and temperamental MGs from half a century or more before, driven or delivered from posh estates and neighborhoods from any number of the states of the union and faraway places and even foreign countries, transported in one way or another to my uncle's shop with the greatest confidence that somehow they would be healed from whatever ailment that had overtaken them.

After my initial week of orientation, I was assigned to a single mechanic for days at a time to learn the ins and outs and soak up some experience and be kind of a Hey Boy around his cubicle, to hand over a screwdriver or hold a flashlight while listening to any number of stories about strange circumstances that had occurred over the years while the storyteller's head was stuck under a bonnet or his body stretched beneath a frame. I spent another week after that learning how to properly wash and detail a car and how to clean it on the inside and have it looking and smelling showroom new when I finished. When it appeared I'd learned my lessons well enough and wasn't a threat to mangle somebody's prized Bentley, I was given my own work area and allowed to perform simple procedures on some of the lesser vehicles, such as changing the oil and replacing worn windshield wiper blades, like I was a surgeon who hadn't made it to the bigtime yet.

November arrived and bad weather came with it, cold rain and dismal, gray skies and northwest breezes that set in after Halloween and wouldn't go away, but instead of business dying down from the dreary conditions, Wright's was instead inundated with torrents of automobiles. Some days I was so busy it seemed like the hours had been whisked away by the newly-arrived winter winds.

Coupled with this phenomenon—which Uncle John assured me was not unusual because a lot of his customers used the winter to pamper and perfect their vehicles so they would be in good order and ready for the coming spring—one of the mechanics failed to show for work on a Monday, and it was discovered later in the afternoon that he had suffered some sort of medical event during the night and died. This was not good news for my uncle, since the deceased Jerry Brannon was his best mechanic at the time and was leaving behind quite a vacancy. Besides the grieving and the funeral—Uncle John actually closed the shop down so every employee could attend the service—there was now the need to find a replacement for Jerry. By Uncle John's high standards, I knew such a thing was not going to be easy.

After Jerry Brannon's death my uncle became more selective about doling out reservations for appointments, since without the leadership of his ace mechanic he was unable to provide the same stellar service in a reasonable amount of time as before, so for three weeks he thinned down service appointments while he searched for a new upscale mechanic to pick up the slack and get production rolling one hundred percent again. Therefore, I and everyone else around the place actually had time to catch our breaths and not feel so harried every minute of the day. This may have been bad for Wright's bottom line, but I could feel a sigh of relief coming from everyone else. It was nice to take it easy, even though the knowledge was there that it wasn't going to last.

Two weeks later, on the day before Thanksgiving, Uncle John closed the shop at noon as had become a custom down through the years so the employees and their families could have a meal on his behalf before breaking for the four-day holiday weekend. Other than being around some of the attendees in a work environment for a few months by then, I had really not formed friendships with any of my associates just yet. I knew them mostly by name and what they'd told me of their past experiences repairing high-end foreign vehicles, but I didn't know who was married and who was not, who had kids and who secretly partied all weekend with drugs and alcohol, or who was gay and who was straight, so I found myself standing apart from several of the conversational circles where people gathered to chat and smile at each other before the vittles appeared and plates could get filled and everyone could begin gorging themselves, standing there alone with my thoughts and a vacant smile on my face like I had some idea where I fit in this particular scheme of things. Like most times in my life, I was clueless.

I guess Uncle John must have felt sorry for me in my plight, for in a matter of minutes he made his way over to my section of the sparkling work-area now turned dining room where I was standing my lonely vigil to see if I was all right. At his side was a woman surpassing gorgeous, recognizable to me as Teresa, my uncle's second wife, younger than him by a couple of decades and maybe twenty years older than me. I'd seen pictures of her before but we'd never met, even though she'd been married to Uncle John for almost fifteen years. She was quite a change from my first aunt, Aunt Mary, who was Uncle John's age and had a while back been sent packing with a trunk of money when Uncle John decided to promote Teresa from shop receptionist to wife. It was a strange kind of feeling for me, to have sudden stampeding lust in my heart overtaking my thoughts for a vintage woman who was technically my aunt. It was like I was dead-set on committing the sin of incest without giving it much of a thought, but one look at my step-aunt and I knew I shouldn't be faulted for at least considering leaping into the gutter and wallowing around a little, for my step-aunt Teresa was really quite the looker.

Uncle David didn't introduce her to me as Aunt Teresa, which was good, because that made it easier to conveniently ignore family ties and out and out feast my eyes on her instead. I wasn't exactly a gentleman in those days. And besides, it wasn't as if I had anything else to do right then but check her out. I certainly wasn't engaged in deep conversation with anyone else at the moment, so I was more than happy to make Teresa's acquaintance, even if I was thinking of her as a good substitute for Mrs. Robinson on the roster of my rampaging fantasies.

"Leonard, I'd like you to meet Teresa. I can't believe you two haven't met before. Teresa, this is Leonard, Bill's son. Leonard's the one I've been telling you about."

The more I looked at the two of them together, the older my uncle looked and the younger Teresa seemed. There was something in me that suggested when we shook hands I should hold on to her fingers as long as I could.

"So you're the new up and coming mechanic, huh?" she smiled.

"I'm here," I said. "I don't know how up and coming I actually am."

"Leonard's coming along fine," Uncle John said.

The two stood there beside me for a polite minute with Uncle John pointing out various dignitaries and pillars of the community who'd dropped by on invitation and named off spouses and children of various employees as if I was interested, while Teresa mainly stood looking like goddamn Rita Hayworth and from time to time inquiring of me how I happened to end up being a mechanic at Wright's Foreign Car Repair. I told the truth about some things, but found it worked out better if I embellished the facts some and beat my brains out trying to make her laugh. Being around a beautiful woman has always turned me from a just the facts kind of dude into Bozo the Clown, even if the beautiful woman happened to be married to my father's brother.

"I went to school planning to be a Baptist preacher, but when I found out cavorting with women and guzzling beer and experimenting with drugs weren't part of the curriculum, I switched over to English Literature and Political Science. I figured with that combination I could be as corrupt as Lord Byron and lie like a politician too, so I thought that might be the ideal lifestyle for me."

Teresa gave me a faint smile and a really fakey chuckle, so I could tell I wasn't going to get too far in the chummy stage with her. She was, after all, way out of any league I'd ever played in. After five minutes or so she strolled off, saying her niece was here and she had to go meet her. By this time Uncle John was busy talking with about a million of the rich and influential people blanketing the place, his pals and partners, so I helped myself to a draft beer from the wet bar and wandered around trying to find a place where I might fit in. There was music playing from a stereo system, some form of light jazz that was simultaneously breezy and semi-somber, and I got it in my mind that as soon as I finished my beer and everyone started chowing down, I would disappear out into the lot and get in my Civic and split. I thought that now that I'd been seen it was safe to steal away while no one was noticing and go to a Sonic and have a foot long with onions, which was more my speed and more in keeping with my dietetic tastes.

I was ten yards away from the door when a hand gripped my arm and one of the mechanics I'd apprenticed under, Scotty Tatum, told me to come on and eat and sit with him, how his wife was out of town and he wasn't too comfortable hanging around with people and their families or strangers he had no idea of who they were and they had no idea who he was either.

"We'll find a place where we can down some turkey and dressing and look at some of these women walking around here. There's some quality stuff in attendance, Leonard, in case you haven't noticed. They're most of them too rich to have anything to do with the likes of me, but it doesn't hurt to look when you get the chance."

I got in line behind Scotty and listened to him tell me jokes that went in one ear and escaped twice as fast out the other. I remembered getting this sort of entertainment non-stop back when it had been my time to work with Scotty, how I'd gotten tired of his stories and one-liners really quick but had nonetheless been amazed as to the way he could do something mechanical that would take a

Rhodes Scholar months to learn how to perform while running his mouth spouting inanities at the same time.

"A guy woke up one morning with a hard-on that wouldn't go away, so after a few hours he decided to go to a walk-in clinic to get help..."

I stopped listening because I was watching my step-aunt over at the dessert table getting cheesecake. She was standing with a younger version of herself, who I guessed had to be her niece. The niece wasn't quite the bombshell Teresa was just yet, but just looking at her from afar I already knew she was one of those girls who gets better looking every time you lay eyes on her. I wondered if there were other women in Teresa's family, or what her mother or her niece's mother must look like, if any of them happened to be Ava Gardner or Loretta Young or somebody like that.

For some reason, all at once I was dying for a slice of cheesecake too. It was like I was a member of Ulysses' crew and there was a siren song in the air I couldn't resist, so I left Scotty in mid-joke and made my way over to the dessert table. I can't say what got into me all of a sudden, if it was the room full of attractive women or the beer I'd downed or what. I'm not generally or almost never have been the kind of guy to aggressively pursue a woman right off the bat the way I did that afternoon, but there I was, full speed ahead with but one thing on my mind. Maybe it was because I'd been removed from feminine wiles for so long during my six weeks at Hannah Hills and the ensuing months afterward living with my parents, but it also could have been that here I was in a new world thinking it was now or never for me to participate in what this land had to offer and that it was up to me to step up to the plate and take a swing if I planned on ever getting on base. It was like all at once I'd had enough of playing second fiddle and sitting out every dance because I was too afraid to open my mouth and ask some dreamboat if she wanted to twirl around the floor with me. I guess I also figured if I struck out in my endeavors I was at least here in the company of strangers and no one would know who the poor sap with desperation etched on his face who'd swung and missed with a comely woman happened to be. Nobody was going to much give too much of a damn what happened to some wretched anonymous stranger in the old romance department this day, if the damn fool fell on his face and lost some teeth in the process or not.

I said hello again to Teresa, who smiled at me and then introduced me to her niece.

"This is Jennifer," she said. "She's my sister's daughter. I'll bet you've seen her before on television."

She was right. I had seen Jennifer Payne on television, but I couldn't remember where or when it was, only that I recognized her from somewhere. It turned out Jennifer was the short-skirted blonde who advertised Mercedes and Jaguars and Land Rovers for a big automobile dealership on television late at night, her with her smile and tight dresses telling the viewers how they needed to improve their lives by buying a spanking new vehicle that cost the moon and stars. Jennifer Payne was one of those visions on TV who kept guys like me from falling asleep during the commercial breaks of Seinfeld reruns.

"Hello, Jennifer. I'm Leonard Wright." I had to tell her my name, since Teresa hadn't bothered to when we were introduced. Maybe she forgot who I was or something, or maybe she didn't think my name was all that important.

"Hello," she said.

I shook her hand and immediately knew I wanted to touch more of her than her palm and a couple of fingers.

"I'm John's nephew," I went on. "I started working here a couple of months ago. I'm not really much of a mechanic, but I suppose I'm as qualified to do this as I am anything else. If you want to know the truth, I'm an English major by trade who refuses to teach. See, I can't stand children, or it could be I'm just selfish. If I know anything worth telling I'd as soon keep it to myself, and that doesn't really transfer to the classroom. Still, in the end I have to do something to make dough and pay the rent. It took me a long time to discover I can't go to movies every night and sleep until noon the rest of my life, so I came to the understanding that foreign car repair might not be too harmful to my health in the long run. I figure maybe somebody rich and powerful will be impressed with my work one of these days and give me a huge stipend I can live on until they're ready to cart me off to a rest home where everybody watches TV all day and retreats way down deep within themselves to where they never will be bothered again, some place like that where I'll feel right at home."

This Jennifer was smiling at me by the time I finished my lengthy and I hoped captivating tirade. It wasn't clear whether she was amused or attracted or thought I was just another nut who was loose this day from the asylum, but she at least didn't try to get away from me like I had a bad case of poison oak. She stood there in her loveliness and took a bite of cheesecake and looked me in the face and smiled.

Boy, she had eyes. Perhaps they were a little fake and maybe she dabbed on the makeup a little much, but she was on TV, man, and I guess that was something a girl had to do when she had to get in front of a camera. She didn't need it though. Even a dumbass like me could see that. She was close enough to movie star-like underneath all that powder and cream and gook. She could have saved her money and done without any of it.

In the freshly scrubbed, spick and span area transformed from a garage, the floors covered with rubber matting and all the vehicles moved around to the back, Wright's spacious floor had become a large banquet room, and as I looked around I saw the invited denizens milling and talking, sitting and flitting, and I thought of how here I was among them, not a rehab admittee or a social outcast any longer, but a member this minute of a higher brand of personage than I'd been a part of ever before. Yes, here I was, standing beside a knockout of a woman, so perhaps there was room for me somewhere in this royal kingdom too.

When Teresa turned away to speak to someone Jennifer came closer and offered a bite of cheesecake to me from the fork she held in her fingers.

"Have a bite," she said. "Tell me if you think it's as delicious as I do."

I tasted the concoction from her fork and made certain I licked the cream from the tongs. I thought how it might be to taste this woman in some similar manner.

"Well, two o'clock," she smiled. "It's time for this girl to go to work. Everyone else might be off for the holiday but I've got a commercial to film. I have to dress up like Santa and sell people cars to put under their trees."

"I've seen your commercials," I said. "If I had the dough, I'd follow you to the dealership right this very minute and buy a sedan or two for myself. Tell your boss the reason their sales are up is probably all your doing. I mean, how can a fellow resist what you tell him?"

"Well now, aren't you a sweetie?" she said.

That got me going even more.

I couldn't believe the line of bull that kept coming out of my mouth, but it was like there was a leak in the dam and there was no stopping the water. I was suddenly in the presence of some dream I'd stored in the back of my head for safekeeping for a long time, and I'd identified it this day when it came near and was outright determined not to let it disappear until I'd blown my horn and sounded the Calvary Charge.

"I guess I'll be seeing you around very soon," she smiled. "I don't see how a man can make so many complimentary statements to a woman if he wasn't interested in seeing her again, so I hope that's the way you feel." She batted her eyes at me—I swear she did, I didn't imagine it—and then she picked up a napkin and held it up. "Have you got something you can write my number down with?"

"No," I said. "I left my Magic Markers at home. Just tell me and I'll remember it. I've got a good memory. Anyway, how in the name of God am I ever going to forget anything you tell me? You're sort of impossible to forget."

Like I say, I was in rare form that afternoon.

She turned to leave, and I went with her. I walked outside to her car, a fairly new Mercedes sedan—my company car, she told me--and glimpsed a flash of her legs when she got in. She gave me a smile and a finger wave and drove away, and I stood there in the lot watching her disappear. It was the day before Thanksgiving, and damned if I wasn't thankful for being alive and well for a change. It was the funniest feeling, altogether strange and unusual, and the November afternoon suddenly seemed to me about as sunny and bright as a Thanksgiving Eve could possibly get.

Although it was still early, I decided to leave the holiday luncheon right then and take a little drive through downtown and see what the city was looking like these days. As I was getting ready to pull out I saw a battered and rusted red Sunbeam Tiger cruising through the lot like it was looking for something. I didn't recognize the driver as anybody I knew, not an employee or a customer I was familiar with, yet I stopped and watched him creep along in his car anyway, like there was going to be a test later. Maybe it was because the Sunbeam was an unusual automobile to be out on the streets of Nashville just then, when the only time I'd much even seen one anywhere before was in the old Get Smart TV show, or maybe watching Liz Taylor crash one on the movie screen in Butterfield 8, or Tuesday Weld tool around in one in Pretty Poison, but I'd never seen one up close in real life that I could remember. I was at least well-versed enough in automobile history to know that the Tiger was a relative of the Sunbeam Alpine, the little number James Bond wound around mountain roads in Doctor No, and of the Talbot, like the one Grace Kelly and Cary Grant cruised through Monaco in during To Catch A Thief, and that when Ford bought the Rootes Groupe out and brought it to America they dropped a V-8 under the hood so it would rival the Cobra. I was familiar enough with them to know that Sunbeam Tigers in their day could fly. The only problem was Ford lost interest in them and sold them off to Chrysler and they went to hell after that. There weren't many of them still on the road, but the ones that were around were worth a pretty penny.

So here was a Sunbeam Tiger, and I watched it come to a stop and a fellow open the door and get out. He walked up to the office door and read the hours of operation posted there and jiggled the doorknob once or twice, like he wasn't sure the place was closed for the holiday or not. I wondered if there was something wrong with his car and he wanted to get it fixed, or if he wanted to bring it by and see if Uncle John might want to buy it from him. That happened a lot at Wright's. People came by with their vintage cars ready to give them up, trying at long last to be a grownup and get rid of those vestiges of their long-ago youths, but still sad in their hearts to think that their love affair with their car was coming finally to an end and the chances were a great romance such as the one they'd experienced with their foreign lover would never come their way again.

I couldn't really get a intimation on this fellow, what it was he wanted or needed to know. I decided to walk over and say something to him, to help him out in whatever he needed from Wright's Foreign Car Repair. It would be like my good deed for the day, me being an ambassador for the company or some such foolishness as that. I could quell my curiosity about his Sunbeam Tiger, ask if he'd owned it a while like I'd once owned my Midget, and if he'd had some wonderful times in it he'd never forget, just like I'd had in my car. Maybe we would have something in common. But I didn't get the chance to speak to him, for he turned away quickly from the door and was back inside the Tiger like he wanted to be alone inside it once again. He shifted into first gear and drove away. Even with my window up and the radio on I could hear the low throaty growl of the V-8 engine from inside that Sunbeam's tiny frame, and in my car as far away as I was I sat for a minute or so listening to the throb of that engine until it faded away. I thought about trying to catch up with him and following behind a while to see where he would go and to listen for a moment to the Tiger's 289, but I knew with me in my Civic and he in his Tiger with the big meaty V-8 the only way I'd ever catch him was if he came to a stop, that if he was on the highway now I could never hope to keep up.

I wondered why he had caught my interest so at just a first glance, and why I couldn't stop wondering if I'd ever see him again.

I couldn't say. It was a mystery.

About a mile from where I grew up is a lengthy stretch of road that leads to a busy intersection that connects to just about every important point in the city of Nashville. If you turn left the road leads to the posh neighborhoods and upscale shops of the west side of the city, where, if you're so inclined, you can buy diamonds or furs or any number of meaningful trinkets anyone from the lesser real world would never think of purchasing, and afterwards you can dine in an upscale restaurant where a cup of coffee costs just below the minimum wage. If you choose to go straight you pass away from most semblances of affluence and travel instead through industrial parks and businesses and detention centers for youths and women and men who commit petty larcenies and possess drugs or knock over liquor stores with unregistered weapons. Off to the right on that venue sits the remains of a state prison that once housed rapists and killers until it closed, wherein it became a movie set and a setting for haunted house tours during Halloween.

Heading east takes you to shops and Centennial Park with its giant statue of Athena and various hospitals and a slew of universities before coming on the downtown section where the road turns into Broadway, and in any direction as far as one can see are honky-tonks and souvenir shops and the arena where the NHL Predators play and big-name concerts are held. Across the street sits the Ryman Auditorium where Country Music first came to life, and down the way is the Cumberland River and the downtown riverfront park and a jillion or so more bars and honkytonks where tourists and citizens gather for Fourth of July and New Year's Eve fireworks and any other pleasure that involves alcohol and war whooping.

And if you go south, you soon leave Nashville and drive toward Brentwood and Franklin, where abundant traces of wealth and affluency appear on a regular basis.

I find this hometown of mine a new and stranger place each and every time I travel through it these days. It's hard to believe that the dingy scum bucket shambles of the Lower Broad of my youth that once only housed peep shows and dive bars and was the habitat of pimps and prostitutes and all manner of homeless and drug-riddled mentally deranged lowlifes is now a mecca for tourism. At the same time, it is also a matter of fascination how rich one burrow of the city can be while the other end wallows in poverty, how the sight of gleaming structures and gated mansions quickly turn to sleezy eyesores in only a matter of miles. Nashville is a city of highs and lows, lies and truths, rights and wrongs, and I have very few ideas where it begins or ends these days, if one portion is more real than another. The longer I hang around the more of a mystery the whole shebang becomes.

At the center of this intersection where all directions point to a different variety of life in their proximity, Wright's Foreign Car Repair occupies a plot of real estate where it has been in operation for more than a quarter of a century. When the morning and afternoon traffic backs up and clogs, a driver can sit in his car for long periods at the intersection and wile away the wait for the light to change by glancing at the big garage and the modern partition where the office and the customer lobby of the business are located and the parking area beside it always filled with all manner of luxury cars and roadsters and coupes with running boards and elaborate hood ornaments, and for a moment a fellow can allow his mind to imagine himself behind the wheel of one of those automobiles cruising down a road to some magnificent gala being held at a sprawling country estate, driving along on a winding mountain byway to a place of riches with perhaps a Daisy Buchanan-type there in the passenger seat beside him, all blonde and breathtaking with the wind in her golden hair, with his hands on the wheel and leaning into the curves while sometimes looking over and smiling in a way at this King's daughter whose very presence says that all is well and this is the way life will hereafter always be.

It was after Christmas that year before I came across two things that would change the landscape of Nashville for me for good. The first was my learning that my uncle was not the righteous totally upright fellow he liked everyone to think he was, that despite the fact he was widely-respected in all his business dealings and lived outside the city limits of Nashville in the richest county in

Tennessee and had a breathtaking wife whose very presence made men tremble and inflicted women with awe-stricken jealousy, that all that was just smoke and mirrors, that apart from all his blessings and earthly riches none of it was enough for him and had never been enough down through the years, not from his college days at North Carolina until thirty-five years later when lodged within the success of his business ventures and the ever-expanding wealth of his assets and the winning of the hand of one of the most beautiful women in the South he had still found none of his treasures enough to hold and entrance him for too long a time. Over the years, I came to learn, my uncle had become involved in other businesses and investments that were not so legitimate as foreign car repair. There was money hidden from sight, and the topper—or at least it seemed so for me at the time—other woman besides his first wife, my real aunt, first Teresa, and then when she assumed the mantle of Mrs. Wright, a string of other women to tarry with after he'd had his fill of her.

The second memorable thing was the arrival of Sam Thornton, the new mechanic Uncle John hired to take the place of Jerry Brannon. Sam Thornton turned out to be the same fellow I'd noticed the afternoon of Thanksgiving Eve, the figure who'd stopped and looked at the hours of operation on the door and driven off in the rusted Sunbeam Tiger with the engine that sounded like a DC-10 at the airport when he sped away.

Uncle John brought Sam around that first Monday in January after the holidays—save for the Epiphany--were finished. I'd seen Sam Thornton drive up that morning in the red Sunbeam with the top that was threadbare in places and duct-taped together in the plastic glass at the back. I already knew someone new had been hired, but hadn't known it was the same man I'd watched from afar those four weeks before. I didn't say anything about it when we were introduced and shook hands. Probably it was none of my business what Sam Thornton drove or where he had come from. I only noticed that he was maybe a quarter century older than me, and I supposed he must have spent his youth hanging out in garages and studying foreign cars and how they worked in order to get this kind of high-paying job at Wright's, where only the elite brought their toys to be repaired and expected the very best expert service in return for the exorbitant amount of cash they shelled out getting it done.

       After a day or two, Sam seemed to single me out among all the other mechanics, possibly because he learned I was the newest member of the company next to him, and because I hadn't been there a thousand years already he thought that perhaps he could talk to me without trying to impress me with his superior expertise. Whenever he took a break from work he'd visit the drink machine by my stall and lean against the wall and ask me how it was going with my oil changes and windshield wiper changing. After three weeks he had already been assigned the majority of the repairs that required an abundance of comprehension and know-how, and I'd taken note of the fact that my uncle seemed to have given Sam free reign from the beginning, acknowledging that Sam knew without hesitation what to do and how to do it and didn't need anyone's input or experience or expertise for assistance. How, I wondered, did this guy learn so much about foreign cars? And how was it that he had come looking for a job with my uncle instead of already having a high position elsewhere, or even owning his own shop somewhere to vie his trade?

       I began probing and poking into his background when I talked to him. If nothing else, befriending such a fellow as Sam Thornton could help me down the road, when the inevitable moment came where I would make a grave mistake and expose myself for the fool I am to everyone. I thought it might be good to have a sort of bodyguard around to cushion the trauma.

       "Tell me about this Tiger you're driving," I said. "How long have you had it? Where did you get it? From everything I've heard, they're hard to find these days."

       "The Tiger's my very first car," he smiled. "I've always had it. I've been driving it since I was fifteen, when I first got my learner's permit. It was my dad's originally, but he died when I was thirteen. I begged my mother not to sell it and we kept it in our garage for a couple of years. I'd take it out to wash and wax and back up and down the driveway in it, and sometimes I'd sneak and drive it around the block if I thought I could get away with it. It was already pretty beat up when I got it and I never have gotten around to getting it painted and pristine, because it seems like every time I get ready to do something like that some disaster comes up and I'm all at once dead broke again." He smiled again and shrugged his shoulders. "My dad died and left the family a lot of bills to pay off, so I never had much of a chance to make it to the top of the financial hill and get the opportunity to roll downhill any. My mother was pretty much an invalid the last five years of her life, so that sucked up a lot of money too. Most of my life's been about being broke for as long as I can remember."

I think this was as much as Sam had ever talked to anybody since he'd come to work at Wright's or probably in a long while too, so I felt lucky in a way, because the way he'd recounted his David Copperfield past made it seem to me like it was a preface to something special yet to come, and it seemed to me that Sam Thornton and I might become fast amigos here at my uncle's shop. He sounded like he was lonesome enough after so many years of scraping by to welcome somebody to confide in, and God knows I was tired of being completely out on my own in the world too. It seemed like forever since I'd had somebody who'd listen to what I said and actually laugh at my weird sense of humor. The truth was I was as lonesome at Wright's Foreign Car Repair as Sam was. It looked to me like we were two loners who were destined to strategically come together.

"Come on," he said after closing time one afternoon. "Let's go for a ride."

I think he'd maybe been thinking of inviting me to go out with him for a drink or two for a few days by then, and all at once I wondered if it could be he was gay and was maybe hitting on me, but that wasn't the case. He just wanted somebody along to take a spin with him.

I stooped down and got into the passenger bucket seat. The Sunbeam reminded me a little of my old Midget, and when I surveyed the dash and the floor shift and the instrument panel I started missing my old girl-catcher, and all at once I knew it was only a matter of time before I was done with my Honda Civic and its plain resourcefulness and practicality. Suddenly I wanted to be a young man again. I wanted to throw my convertible top back and look up at the sky and feel the wind in my face and hear the hum of tires on pavement while I cornered turns and saw the world go by with a renewed vision I'd believed for a while had been taken from me forever.

All this was going on in my head as I sat as a passenger in Sam Thornton's beat-up Sunbeam Tiger. It was old and rusted and the seats were frayed and had holes in the vinyl here and there, and it was only a glimmer of the car it used to be, but the engine growled and the four-speed thrust it forward with a jerk, and the car and Sam Thornton were in a world free and new and I wanted to be there too. I wanted to visit that world in my own two-seater.

After thirty minutes of blasting up and down the interstate and around city streets with tour busses and entertainment rides hauling drunken partygoers down Broadway and downtown, we crested a hill and came to a stop at a upscale pub and went inside to sit and drink beer and eat chicken wings and watch through the front window women in winter garb walk up and down the street, looking like products of our dual imaginations, so pretty and doll-like we dared not think about going near and touching them for fear we would spoil and mar their beauty somehow by doing so, like we were neither of us worthy to be involved with them outside the imaginary scheme of things in our heads, as if our physical presences would do nothing but ruin the landscape.

"Look but don't touch," Sam laughed. "That's been the story of my life so far."

"They're not real anyway," I concurred. "Once you get within three feet of them they dissolve and disappear back into Fantasyland. Most of them have staple marks in their bodies anyway, because they only exist in Playboy Magazine."

I started to offer more about the injustices of my romantic fortunes so far in my life, but I stopped all at once in mid-sentence when I saw my step-aunt Teresa and her niece Jennifer come in the door. Teresa and Jennifer were certainly show-stoppers this early evening, and I saw Sam staring at the two of them the same way I was.

"Before you say anything or sell your soul to the devil," I told him, "I already know who those two are. One's an aunt and the other is her niece. Jennifer and Teresa. Jennifer's the younger one. The other woman is her aunt, who also just happens to be the wife of our very own employer, and therefore technically my aunt. Teresa Payne-Wright—that's her name. Small world we live in, don't you think?"

We were sitting at a table in front of the two women by the doorway, so it wasn't any surprise when Jennifer looked over and saw us. Something in her eyes lit up and made me want to hop up from my seat and run over to her and beg for attention like I was a starving dog or something, but I contented myself to simply smiling and lifting my hand from my wings platter and offering a wave.

She touched Teresa on the shoulder and they both walked toward us. If I'd ever doubted God loved me I knew for sure at that moment in time He certainly did.

"Imagine seeing you here," Jennifer smiled. "I didn't think you ever left work at all, that maybe you were afraid Mr. Wright would fire you if you went anywhere outside his web of supervision. At least that's the reason I gave myself for you not calling me like you said you would."

She sat down in the chair beside me, her delicious hip brushing mine as she settled in.

"Oh, I imagine John doesn't have to watch him anymore," Teresa said. "Like everyone else at the shop, Leonard is perfectly house-trained and a genuine member of the team by now. There's not a soul there who would step out of line for the life of them, and he's right there with them. Everyone's brainwashed, so they're not even capable of any acts of disloyalty." She looked over at Sam and smiled. "I'm the only person my dear husband ever has to worry about whatsoever."

"You're his wife," Jennifer laughed. "You're not classified as an employee."

"Oh, but to John Wright, a wife and an employee are much the same. Each has a position and purpose and it all has to mesh smoothly to further his cause." She set her bag down on the floor by her feet and took off her jacket. She smoothed out her dress with her fingers and looked Sam's way. "I'm Teresa Payne-Wright," she said, "and you are...?"

"Sam Thornton."

Sam said his name abruptly, without any flourish or fanfare at all. It was like there was no need to bother with embellishments.

"You're John's new wunderkind, aren't you? His master mechanic he's managed to bring on to save the floundering ship?"

"I don't know if I'd quite describe it that way, but yes. I'm the new hired hand. Me and Leonard here are the new kids on the block."

Teresa seemed to look at him for a long moment, and for a heartbeat it was as if Jennifer and I had been regulated to a distant room so Teresa and Sam could have this moment to themselves. I didn't quite know what I was thinking or any way to put it into words, but there was something in me that said not to forget this flash of insight that had come my way just now, because someday it would come back to me as one of those times in life when something rare was blossoming and anything seemed possible.

Teresa began talking about the recent Christmas holidays and how she had been to New York to shop and see some plays. I took it that this was an annual event for her and that my uncle was not invited to go along on these jaunts, and Teresa was quick to assure us how John had never made any kind of trip with her during their marriage and how their union had always been defined by each of them having the space and the right to go and do whatever they pleased with no strings attached.

"Right from the beginning John made it clear how he had a life to himself and nothing was ever going to change that. Once I became accustomed to the idea, it worked out for me too. These days the two of us simply pass like ocean liners in the Atlantic, making certain there's plenty of room between us so we can get to where we want to be." She took a sip of wine and smiled and turned her face toward Sam. "I suspect, though," she said, "that my husband may have accidentally booked himself on the Titanic and hasn't realize it yet, and someday an iceberg is going to come along and he'll be looking for a lifeboat and there won't be any room."

From then on, it was like the four of us had paired off at a high school party, Jennifer and me, Sam and Teresa, each of us saying what we thought we should to further our causes, holding in our secret hearts the thrilling thought of being somehow alone with the person beside us, wishing and praying the stars would align and fate would not allow us to do something to keep our greatest desires from happening. By this time the building was filled to its capacity, and people stood in the doorway waiting for a table to free up. I looked at my watch and was astounded to find we'd been sitting at our table for hours.

Now, being drunk is not a new thing with me. I was a frat boy at the University of Tennessee, you see, so being lit and slobbered to the gills is a pretty familiar feeling. It wasn't like I was physically right then in any kind of different place than I'd been a couple of thousand times in the past, but what was astounding to me this night was the rare company I was keeping, Jennifer Payne the luscious spokesperson who was eye candy for luxury cars, Teresa, married to my father's rich brother, and Sam Thornton, my new best friend of a few days now, my cohort at Wright's and the owner of the sad and rusted Sunbeam Tiger he drove each day as a remembrance of who he'd once been and where he had come from and how someday he would find the means to restore both the car and his lost and lonely soul to a place among the bright world he'd not yet found a way to enter into.

I was drunk all right.

"I don't know your husband very well," Sam said to Teresa. I looked at him and unlike the rest of us, he appeared deathly sober, as if he hadn't been sitting at this table for hours drinking draft beer as fast as the smiling fellow in the black apron could bring it. "That being said, I can't imagine him being all that pleased with his new mechanic and his nephew wiling away the evening with his wife and her niece, the four of us having the best of times while he's sitting at home in his den watching Sportscenter all by himself."

"Oh, I doubt very seriously John is alone," Teresa said. "John is never alone. You can go to the bank on that. He hasn't spent a single night alone in a long time. He's always got plenty of company, and I certainly don't mean just me."

"If you want to observe the workings of an open marriage, all you have to do is drop by 128 Windsor Lane," Jennifer laughed.

"You can have your eyes opened pretty fast by what you see and don't see there." She turned to me and smiled. "It's not like Lucy and Ricky at all."

"It's not as bad as it sounds," Teresa smiled. "As a matter of fact, about everybody I know is jealous they don't have a relationship like ours. Most of my friends despise the person they're married to and would love to have the same opportunities I have."

"I haven't ever been married," I said, "so I wouldn't know."

"I started to get married once," said Jennifer, "but I guess I came to my senses just in time."

"I talked you out of it, honey," Teresa corrected. "I didn't want you to ruin your life."

"I never got married either," Sam said. "My dad died when I was a kid, and my mother wasn't ever the same after that, so I don't remember much about the family unit gathering around the dining room table on holidays or much of any other time. I spent Thanksgiving on the school playground shooting basketball while all my friends were at Grandma's having dinner."

We hadn't noticed it happening, but outside the rain had turned to sleet and the walkway and the shrubs lining it was beginning to ice over. The pub began to thin out a little, the patrons getting in their cars and driving home while they still could. It was funny somehow. It hadn't seemed so cold earlier in the evening. During our ride in the Sunbeam and while we'd been sitting inside I'd felt warm and contented. Now I thought of driving back to get my car and how I'd have to navigate the ride home on icy streets while being four sheets to the wind. I didn't want to wreck the Civic or get pulled over by the cops. If I had my way, I'd just keep sitting here beside Jennifer Payne listening to stories about open marriage and holidays and what made everybody happy and how they made it through life every day. I'd just sit and listen, because I didn't much want to go into the stuff about losing my job and Hannah Hills and my enrollment in rehab and twelve steps and all that crap I'd found myself doing because I was a failure when it comes to living a fruitful life.

Teresa was the first to make mention of the winter storm going on outside. She touched Jennifer on the hand and pointed out the window at the white curtain of snow and ice falling. I'd been hoping she wouldn't notice, that no one would, and our evening together would just go on no matter what sort of curveball nature was throwing us.

"I suspect we'd better be ambling along," Teresa said. "I'm afraid if we hang around too much longer we might not make it home before sunrise." She smiled as she fished her car keys from her purse. "Of course, that wouldn't make much difference around Windsor Lane. Not too many nights pass when I or my charming husband are both home by that time of the day anyway. Lots of times we make other sleeping arrangements."

She looked at Sam so directly that I knew he'd have to be a fool not to sense the implications of that remark. Just the idea of Teresa sleeping somewhere other than her own bed stirred something inside me, made my senses prick to consider such a scenario. This vision in my head didn't shock me that much though, being as I am an inveterate dreamer who lives in a fantasy world as I have forever enjoyed doing.

Sam got it all right, I could tell, but he didn't reply. He walked over to the cashier and paid our bill. We'd been there so long and ate and drank so much I knew the total had to be astronomical and enough to choke a horse. I thought I should go over and offer to pay my share of it, but who was I kidding? I was sitting there broke as Joe's turkey. I wouldn't have any cash until payday, which was still two days off.

Outside on the porch, we said our goodnights and started to head to our vehicles to go home. Sam made it a point to escort Teresa and Jennifer toward Teresa's Mercedes, a shiny black little number with patches of snow beginning to cling to its roof and hood. He brushed off her windshield with the sleeve of his jacket and we stood there getting frozen and wet until they drove away. I was drunk enough that it didn't bother me. I was still warm all over from sitting beside Jennifer Payne and looking across at my dreamboat of an aunt for an entire evening, so the snow and freezing rain was going to have to work some to get to me too much. I did wonder why we were still standing out in the elements, why we didn't trudge over to Sam's Tiger and get the heater going and head for home ourselves.

"Are we just going to stand out here until we turn into snowmen?" I asked.

"I didn't want your aunt to see what I was driving," Sam said. "A woman like her puts a lot of stock in material things. Here she's driving a new Mercedes and she'd see me with a run-down rusted sports car that hasn't seen new paint since Jimmy Carter was voted out of office. My image is bad enough already, me being one of her husband's flunkies, so there's no reason to show her what poor and destitute looks like up close. She probably had to read Oliver Twist when she was back in high school, and I didn't feel like re-enacting it for her tonight, making her feel sorry for all the poor unfortunates in the world."

"I don't think she would have done that. I thought they were both pretty damn friendly the whole night."

"Yeah, maybe so." He turned the key and the engine made a tired hesitant groan, then fired up and came to life. He turned on the wipers and they crawled across the glass like they were taking their last breath before going on to the great beyond. Air came out of the vent in a pitiful zephyr of a breeze, and I wondered how long it would take before it was actually warm. I remembered my Midget, and how it would never get toasty in icy weather like this.

"There's one thing I'm wondering about," Sam said. He turned down the radio to make sure I heard him. "I wonder what was going on in Teresa's mind the whole time we were there. Was she just out having fun where she found it, or was she thinking about something else the whole time? Maybe she was remembering something she'd forgotten a while back. And I wonder if she liked me the way she acted like she did? She was certainly giving off some strange signals."

"It's hard to tell what a woman is thinking sometimes," I said, expert that I am. "Especially if she's beautiful and been around enough to know some things."

"And rich," Sam said. "Don't forget rich. Rich somehow makes you smarter."

"Yeah, rich," I repeated. I was drunk and I'd agree with anything. "Rich," I said again. "Definitely rich."

Three

Winter began to melt. Business at Wright's not only remained brisk but with the sunshine appearing on a regular basis and a new master mechanic on board the number of cars brought in for service increased. In the overflowing shop, roadsters and town cars and limos came and went and were replaced by more vehicles, expensive and rare and brought in from far-reaching counties and states on their own or on the back of delivery trucks. Once, I saw a Bentley delivered from Switzerland, shipped to Nashville to be gone over because of Wright's elite reputation. Until then, I had never thought such things were feasible. I had not known wealth like this existed in the world, or that it was something of a commonplace these days for the rich to transport their toys and passions to wherever they wished, or how money was never even factored into any such decisions.

On Friday afternoons Sam and I would regularly load up in his Tiger and go to Happy Hours at any number of revolving bars on the stretch of road that connected Nashville and the satellite city of Brentwood and the neighboring town of Franklin. As we motored south, we passed a variety of posh mansions owned by current and past well-to-do citizens in this richest part of the state. We'd drive by the governor's mansion and the estates of politicians and newspaper owners and manicured parks and huge churches and even the house where Hank Williams lived until he turned up dead on New Year's Day a half century before, and when we crossed the county line it was as if schools were all at once larger and more private and houses were farther off the road and high stone fences separated the passers-by in traffic from the dwellings where the superior and elite stayed when they wished to be away from the huddled masses. Finally we would come upon a strip of restaurants and movie houses and cafes and choose one to frequent to escape the dingy world of the working class we'd left behind those fifteen miles back down the road.

And during those nights I listened to Sam spin tales of the world he'd left behind in the years past and hear the music from Sirius swim in my head and watch the women and the wait staff pass by while I swallowed enough Guinness to make me want to join in singing along with the choirs of life going on around me and in the deep imaginative recesses of my mind.

I wasn't nearly as pitiful in my status in the world by then as I'd been a few months before. I had actually screwed up enough courage to call Jennifer Payne a few days after our meeting and ask her out for dinner. That first night I went to a recording studio and waited in the lobby for her while she finished up filming a commercial, and soon our meetings became something of a regular undertaking; two or three nights a week we would go somewhere and eat a sandwich at a place that didn't cost an arm or a leg. She suggested this sort of ritual herself, and I always wondered if she was taking pity on me for being a poor boy or if she herself didn't really care or desire to continually frequent the palaces of the privileged her aunt was constantly dragging her into when they met. Unlike Sam, I didn't mind if Jennifer knew what kind of car I drove or how my economic status might not be what she was accustomed to, because I knew I wasn't much of an actor and had no skills in subterfuge and that the truth about me would come out sooner or later, so I didn't see any need to hide the facts from the start. Yes, I was from the working class, but no, I was hoping not to remain a member of that sect forever. I was hoping my intellect and what I was learning every day at Wright's might somehow work in my favor and elevate me to a higher social sphere. I wanted her to believe I was a person on the rise.

I think my strategy must have somehow been working, because on our fourth late-night dinner together we ordered coffee and sat and talked a long while instead of going home. During the course of that conversation Jennifer told me about her mother's death from cancer when she had only been fourteen, and how her Aunt Teresa had semi-adopted her and looked after her until she finished college at NC-Wilmington. She later disclosed that Teresa and Sam were now seeing each other on a pretty regular basis, and although she had never thought much of her aunt's frequent extra-marital dalliances, this time she could sense that there was something more going on. She wanted to know if Sam had said anything to me about the two of them, and I told her truthfully no, he had not. I was the one who hadn't known such an affair was happening, which upon reflection, was a continuing pattern for me, because being blind to the facts of life has perpetually been a character trait on my part. I seem to only see what I want to see, and if something comes up that promises to become a crisis or rock my boat in the calm little sea I'm floating in, that's when I turn the other way or open a book or head off to a movie to immerse myself in a distant world where real-life drama isn't rising up to my waist and threatening to pull me under its waters and drown me because I don't know how to swim or even tread the rising flood.

Later, after I'd taken Jennifer home that evening, I drove to my house thinking about my step-aunt and my new best pal Sam Thornton and good old Uncle John. On that late night drive it occurred to me that none of my original impressions of any of these people was anywhere near the truth.

When I got home I didn't go straight to bed, even though the next day was a work day and there would be no lounging around for me. Instead of sleeping, I chose to sit in the rocking chair by the window in my boyhood bedroom at my parents' house and stare out at the darkness and the one streetlight that supposedly kept the burglars away, as if there was anything in our residence actually worth stealing. I was certain there was nothing of mine that had any value. The robbers could take my Honda and maybe sell it for parts, but that was about it. I didn't have anything else anyone could possibly desire. I had my clothes and a few books, but they'd net practically nothing at the Salvation Army. My cassette tapes and CDs from high school and college were strewn who knows where and my mother had thrown out my baseball card collection years ago, the only possession I'd owned that would be of any value these days. I wasn't like other people in the world—I wasn't working a hot-shot job and bringing in a wad of dough every week, and I wasn't acting like some reckless character in a movie, conducting illicit affairs and living life on a high wire with danger and drama and everything else being a real-life grownup brought to a person. No, I was just this overaged kid still locked within his singular place where all he did was watch what the other denizens of the planet were doing all around him. It was like I'd not scraped up enough dinero or gumption to pay my admission into an adult existence just yet. I was still out on the fringes in my bleacher seat watching the action and trying the whole while to figure out what the hell was going on and how I could ever join in on the world of real life.

I sat like that a long time until I finally woke with a start and found I'd been dozing. It was three in the morning. I wandered over to my bed and climbed beneath the sheets my mother laundered for me every week, tried to picture an answer on the dark shadows of the ceiling, then mercifully passed out.

Despite my unease, I still somehow managed to awake the next morning with a new sort of resolve in my head. I decided to be a watcher no more in this life, so I embarked on a new rule of order of minding my own business and making sure I was taking steps toward becoming a legitimate member of the world as a dues-paying adult. I decided not to spend any more time wondering about Uncle John and his marital infidelities or how he wasn't the fellow I'd always been told he was, because in the end he lived in a different society from me and was a million miles away from how I had remembered him when I was a boy. I appreciated the Midget he had gifted me long ago and how it had saved me from an uneventful high school experience, and I was thankful too for the job opportunity he had afforded me now, but really, I told myself, that was as far as it went. I had no more of a right to peer into his private affairs as he might have of looking into mine.

I also didn't think it was any of my business to know what was going on with Sam and Teresa. I certainly didn't have any need to protect the family name by coming between my step-aunt and Sam, since they were both older than me and knew a lot more about what they were up to in the grand scheme of the world than I did. Also, it wasn't like I considered Teresa a real member of our family, even if she was married to my uncle. Hell, Teresa was so damned good-looking that if the chance had been there for me to get anywhere with her I'd have been all over her in a second, and that's not really a civilized way a guy should act with a family member. Well, maybe and maybe not. I have to take into consideration that Teresa was simply a woman who was way out of my league, and if I was to start dealing with her sexually it would probably result in either my death or the utter destruction of my faculties. What I'm saying is I don't think at the tender age of twenty-eight I was man enough to handle a woman like her.

Might as well tell the truth.

It was hard, though, for me to go to work every day and see Sam and know what he had likely been up to the night before, and then to see Uncle John when he made his bi-weekly appearances and walked around talking to all his employees and taking care of whatever problems might have arisen since the last time he was here, and I would have to plaster a smile on my face like I was a pure simpleton who had no idea what murky levels of living and loving were going on out in the big bad world. It was difficult to play dumb all the time, but after a while it got to where it was sort of a test and an adventure for me. I wanted to see exactly how stealthy I could be in my day-to-day dealings with the world. Could I keep my taciturn expressions frozen on my face for an interminable period of time? Could I be this undercover espionage-type who kept himself busy in the background gathering information and storing away knowledge to a maximum point while never revealing anything to any of the parties being observed and formulated? Was it possible for me to know more about these people and the roles they played in the sinister world than even they did, so that in the end I would be the one who would know more about the nitty gritty of adult life than any of them?

· · · ·

After another few weeks Sam came up to me at the shop and wondered if I'd like to go have a few beers after work that afternoon. We'd gone a couple of weeks not making our usual rounds—I suppose it was because he was busy with Teresa—and we had a little catching up to do. Maybe he was curious about how it was going with me and the enticing Jennifer. But the way it came to me later was he had so much stored up inside himself that he had to let some of it out or he'd explode. I think what he wanted was someone to listen to his story and not make any kind of suggestion or judgment along the way, and that was exactly the kind of thing I was good at. Nodding my head and not offering any comment was the way I made it through life on a regular basis.

We hunkered down at a not-so-fancy tavern in downtown Nashville and ordered cheeseburgers and fries and informed the lady waiting on us, if she'd please, to keep the pitchers of draft beer coming.

"I suppose you know what I've been up to the last couple of weeks," he offered as a starter.

"Well, I wasn't certain. I didn't know how much you were seeing Teresa until Jennifer mentioned it to me. To tell you the truth, I was hoping you were busy doing something else. Fooling around with your boss's wife, you know, is sometimes not the best path to travel."

"Heck, Leonard, I wasn't planning on anything going on with Teresa. If she hadn't been who she was to begin with none of what's happening would have ever gone down."

I wasn't entirely grasping what he was saying, but somehow I knew that there was more to this romantic liaison than what was appearing on the surface.

"See, what you don't know," Sam said, looking into the depths of his glass, "is that when Teresa and Jennifer first saw us that night that wasn't the first time I'd ever been with Teresa Payne. I can't say I ever really knew her that well, but I'd had some doings with her a long way back. Maybe it wasn't enough to instill any everlasting memory of me in her own brain, but now she's come to remember me and her and a night we spent together a long time ago."

He took a minute to smooth out a napkin in front of him, like he was making sure there were no wrinkles present to make it appear used. He reached over and turned a ketchup bottle around and read the label, then took another swallow of beer before going on.

"That night when we all met, she didn't remember me at first," Sam said. "When she and Jennifer sat down with us it took her the better part of the evening before it dawned on her that she'd seen me before. It wasn't like that with me at all. I knew her from the second she walked in, but I told myself not to say anything, to let things ride for a while and see what happened. It had been thirty years or so since we'd run across each other, and most folks, like you know, have trouble recalling things that happened to them the day before and last week. Not everybody's like me, Leonard, or you too—whether you admit it or not, you remember every little thing that's ever happened to you in your life, and you carry it around while you're trying to act like nothing in the past or anything that comes along right now matters much. You'd rather let everybody else tell their harrowing horror stories of their traumatic lives while you listen and smile and urge them on, because if they're the ones doing all the talking then you don't have to bare your soul or admit to anything that's going to make you look like a lowlife or one of those folks that don't deserve to be where they are."

"Glad you've been able to get me pegged and pigeonholed."

"Hell, I mean it as a compliment. It's the reason I like talking to you so much and telling you crap I wouldn't dare mention to anyone else. It's because you've been there before too. You can be trusted to mind the hot stove because you've been burned a few times yourself."

"Third degree burns," I assured him. "I hurt to this very day."

The jukebox up front was playing Johnny Cash. Earlier I'd heard Emmylou Harris. I settled in and made myself comfortable.

"Like I say, it was a lot of years ago. I was a senior majoring in Philosophy and English at this little burg of a school across the Mississippi River in Arkansas—Landis College, it was a little Liberal Arts place that turned out teachers mostly—and I was financing my way through school by selling assorted drugs on the quiet, on campus and back across the bridge at what was then called Memphis State University. I'd gone there my freshman year and then transferred, so I knew some people and where a lot of the hot spots in Memphis were, places where I could peddle my wares and make some money. The sad thing about it was I was using recreationally a great deal too, so my profits were sometimes pretty miniscule to be taking such a risk. But when you're young it's hard to understand things all the way to the core, and so I kept on and I took a few too many chances than I would have if I'd been playing it smart. But it didn't occur to me that I could have money and have fun while I was doing illegal shit all at the same time and that trouble might come along as a result. I had no idea what the consequences were."

He shook his head and took a glance at my face to see if I was still paying attention, thinking perhaps how maybe I was just another young smartass and wasn't capable of listening to the voice of experience for more than a minute or two, but I suppose he could tell I hadn't tuned him out so far, and so he continued.

"Teresa Payne was a sophomore that year, and it was just after classes started for the fall that I began seeing her around at different places, noticing her, it seemed, like every time I turned a corner or walked across campus, there she'd be. She was generally hanging around with a bunch of other girls—I guess they were dormmates or something like that--so I never saw her by herself those first couple of weeks. Of course, the old adage is that sometimes you can't see for looking, because in a couple of weeks I discovered she was in one of my classes—Shakespeare Tragedies, which I took as an elective that last year just to keep my hours up so I wouldn't have to worry about getting drafted. Viet Nam was going on then—you wouldn't know much about that, you're such a baby— but it was scary stuff for guys in school back in the day. All it took was one fuckup with your grades and suddenly you were caught up in a spiral and there was all kinds of pressure to get your hours and your GPA up so you could stay in school and not be fair game to the Pentagon, which was in need of more warm bodies to serve as cannon fodder and keep the industrial powers up and prosperous. Unless you were a pure genius or your daddy was fucking rich it was a scary time for every male past the age of eighteen."

He motioned for another pitcher of beer and leaned back in the booth.

"Shakespeare Tragedies wasn't that popular a class, and they held it in this big drafty room no one ever used and everyone would spread out in desks and not be crowded in the least. Well, I wasn't all that bold and brave in those days, so when I finally saw Teresa was a member of the class I didn't up and try to scoot in and sit close to her and impress her with my intellect and winning personality. It was more a case of me sitting on the other side of the room with my book opened up to Mercutio getting himself speared by Tybalt and at the same time sneaking looks across the rows at her with her hair down to her ass and that face that simply wouldn't let you stop staring at it. I didn't make any moves on her, but I did study her enough so there wasn't too much left for further memorization. I didn't plan on going any further in my admiration for Teresa Payne at that point. I wasn't stupid, and I'd already determined this was a girl who was way out of my sphere and could only exist for me via my wildest dreams. Well, Leonard, let me be the first to tell you if you don't know already--sometimes God up in Heaven gets bored and needs to have a laugh as much as anybody else--so since He's sitting up there on His throne with all that power and enough idle time anytime He wills it, I guess the temptation to amuse Himself can be damn overwhelming, and so it must have been that way back then with Him and me and my attraction to the celestial Miss Payne. God, I suppose, wondered what might happen if He arranged the chips to fall a certain way and for me and Teresa to make each other's acquaintance, so that's the way He willed it to happen."

I sat there in my cushioned side of the booth, nestling in like a child whose grandfather has started to tell him a bedtime story, and it came to me how Sam was maybe old enough to be my father. I mean, he didn't really seem that age chronologically, but he did possess enough wisdom about the ways of the world and might have seen enough of life by this time that he could even be eighty or ninety, even though I knew he was a lot younger than that. He wasn't decrepit yet for sure.

"I lived with two other jokers in an apartment about a football field away from Landis, and sometimes in the early evenings I'd go over to the boys' dorms and see if anybody was interested in buying a nickel bag or a lid, nothing altogether psychedelic and mind-expanding, mind you, but something maybe you could roll a couple of joints up with and you and your buddies could get off on for a couple of hours. It wasn't like I was dealing with stuff that was going to lead anybody down a labyrinth of madness and never allow them the opportunity to make it back.

"Well, one night when I'd finished making my rounds I ran across a group of kids sitting around the courtyard outside one of the girls' dorms—Wyatt Manor was what they called it, gave it kind of a fancy name so the girls who stayed there thought they were some kind of royalty or something, when in reality they were jammed into a building four to a room over three floors because Landis was money-hungry and enrolled as many students as they could pack in, and crowded conditions were the norm for all the living quarters. But anyway, there a bunch of folks sat milling around, guys and girls shooting the bull and wondering whether to begin performing mating rituals right there on the spot, and I walked up and stopped because I happened to know a couple of the guys and I wanted to be congenial and all that, thinking this was a good chance to sell a little more weed before I went home for the night.

"Now I have to explain that I was just as interested in women as anybody else on the planet at that time, and there were some nice-looking Landis coeds sitting out there in that yard area mingling around, and it turned out Teresa Payne was one of them. I already knew in my head that whether I had any buyers for my services or not that night, I wasn't about to leave until I had the chance to look Teresa over a little more and maybe even talk to her some, which would have been a huge improvement over my gazing at her from afar from across a room for a semester and wondering if she was as good up close as she was from a distance. I wasn't about to split the scene until I'd determined the answer to that burning question.

"See, Leonard, I was half in love with her already by this time. I don't know if you've ever had any such occurrence happen to you in your life before, but I was at that point even with only seeing her from fifty feet away. I'd already come to believe she was the answer to every prayer I'd ever directed toward a female. She was like the symbol of any trophy I'd ever want to win in the Great Romantic Quest of my youth, and there wasn't any logical thinking that was going to deter me from living out my dreams the best I could muster. So I stood and talked and laughed and grinned and inched closer to be nearer to her, and finally I was beside her and talking to her, and lo and behold, the unimaginably impossible thing happened—she recognized me from our Shakespeare class together and we suddenly had common ground to share. It was like

God had given me a great gift, had thrown me a bone when I really needed something to chew on. I blinked my eyes and I could see Him standing off a little way from us, winking at me, mouthing the words that this was my big chance, so don't blow it, urging me on to jump right in.

"In a little while, six or seven of us took off for somebody's apartment, which was a couple of streets over from mine. That area around Landis was like a ghetto in those days, run-down and rotten and rat-strewn, but it was still a treat to a lot of kids living away from home for the first time to be there in a place where there weren't any rules or regulations, where someone could put on some albums and bring out a couple of joints and there'd be wine in the refrigerator, and all at once it's a party and everyone's a grownup and adult all at once. I was no stranger to any of this kind of rebellion by then, because I was a year or two older than anybody there, but not so old that I didn't remember how it was when all the taboos came down and a guy was at last finally on his own to do whatever he pleased.

"Somehow or another, as God had deemed it, Teresa and I found ourselves paired off together and at each other's side, drinking wine and toking on a joint each time it got passed our way. A bong came out and we sampled that too. Music played and we were both pretty high. I remember talking about a lot of stuff with her, Shakespeare and the crazy world and how one day I was going to go out and do this and that, outstanding but fictional exploits, and then I remember she was in my arms and we were kissing and holding each other about as tight as we could, and yes, she was as I'd imagined. She was a dream I hoped I'd never wake up from."

The jukebox up front was playing America. "Sister Golden Hair." I recognized it as Classic Rock, something from the deep past, but I knew to Sam it was from a time he'd once lived in.

"What happened is we made out for a long time," Sam said. "Hours. It was close to midnight when we left. I drove her back to campus in the Sunbeam and walked her up to her dorm. I kissed her goodnight and everyone went inside and I drove back home. I never saw her again until a lot of years went by, and didn't meet up with her until the night you and I met her and Jennifer by chance. For a while she didn't remember who I was, it had been such a long time back.

"The reason there was such a time lapse, see," he explained, "was because I got my ass arrested."

We ordered our last pitcher of the evening and Sam went on with the gristly details.

"The cops were waiting on me that night when I got home. They'd already come in and busted my two roommates for possession and distributing—pot and speed—and they'd waited around for me to turn up so they'd have a full-scale joint arrest under their belts. That way they could release it to the press to show everybody what a hot-shot job they were doing keeping the city clean. I walked in with a couple of lids in my pocket and they tied us all in together, like we were an international drug ring that was bringing the entire city to its knees. I didn't have the money to hire a big lawyer to get me off the hook, so I ended up having to take the plea deal they offered me, which was a $5000 fine and six months in jail. I didn't have to go to a maximum-security prison, but just served my sentence at the city's workhouse, where I went out six days a week picking up trash and getting assigned shitty work details that no person in their right mind would ever think of doing. But I did my sentence and actually got out a month early for being a good boy while I was locked up, but the damage was done even if my sentence got shortened. The five grand I had to pay in fines took my entire life savings and then some, so I had to find a job quick and pay the rest of it off or go back to jail. I couldn't go back to school at Landis because I was a convicted felon and they really frowned on shit like that. I did go by to try and see Teresa again and she wasn't there anymore; she'd transferred somewhere or dropped out and no one knew what to tell me. The people who'd known her sure as hell didn't want anything to do with a drug pusher, so that was a blind alley I had no way of negotiating. I also found out that places of business weren't exactly begging for ex-cons to come work for them, so I had to leave town and make inquiries at every Podunk spot on the map looking for work. There wasn't much of a demand for ex-Philosophy and English majors, so I turned my attention to one of the other things I happened to be good at, which was automobile repair. I could fix cars and always had been able to do so—I guess I learned it from age thirteen fooling around with my daddy's Sunbeam. I studied that manual and read books on car engines and how they worked for years when I was a kid, and before I started college I was as good a mechanic as anybody around. Every mechanic in town who had a shop wanted to hire me, but I was dead-set on going to college and doing something wonderful with my life later on. I was determined to get out of the poor house my family and I had lived in for so long, and when my mother died my freshman year of college I decided to get through school and out into the world the best way I could, and that was when selling drugs became an option. I guess I could have found a regular job and worked my way through school a little at a time, but like I say, I was in a hurry to get out in the world and start living this big technicolored golden life I'd promised myself I'd one day have. And there was also the Draft to worry about.

"You know, Leonard," he said, pausing to look me in the eye to see if I was bored or not, "I never meant anybody any harm in what I did. I never sold anybody anything that I wasn't doing myself. I just wanted to make money to pay the bills and have fun along the way. I was a kid and didn't think anything about what might happen if I screwed up. I really thought I was too smart to get caught, and I was, but it was the two dudes I was living with that didn't have any idea how to be careful or discreet. They went down and pulled me down with them.

"But being locked up, being in jail with all those damn low-lifes and losing everything I had taught me to never trust anybody from then on, just to do things my own way in my own time and see if I could ever get back in the race again. I took jobs working on cars in a number of towns, jumping to places like Louisville and Bristol and Tullahoma, and finally to Nashville, still driving the Tiger all the while, the only thing I had left from thirty-five years of wandering. I took a job at a Goodyear in Nashville fixing engines and installing new tires. On a Saturday I saw where a sports car show was being held out toward Franklin and I drove out to see it. There were all kinds of Jags and Triumphs and Healeys sitting around in a lot, cars I'd worked on before and had a lot of knowledge about since my early days of studying and restoring the Sunbeam, and as I walked around looking everything over I happened to see this guy and a woman standing by the tent headquarters talking to the people working the booth. I stood there for a long minute staring, not believing what my eyes were showing me.

"It was Teresa standing there beside your uncle. She was older and wearing sunglasses and a sunhat covering her hair, but I could see the slope of her nose and the way she stood there like she was outside of it all and was only visiting from some far enchanted land, and I knew immediately it was her. We weren't at Landis College and it wasn't the 1970s but there she was right in front of me, a thousand years and a million miles down the road from when I'd known her before, far removed from the way back when of our two lives, but right there on that day standing twenty feet away for me to see once more.

"I didn't approach her, but watched her out of the corner of my eye and followed the man she was with and her around the show for a while and out into the lot when they were ready to go. They got into a big Cadillac and drove away, and I followed behind like I was a private eye tailing them, all the way to this huge place in Franklin, which was a big antebellum house with columns on the porch and all that kind of jazz, where you might expect Hattie McDaniel to come out on the porch and shake off the parlor rugs or something. I memorized the number on the stone mailbox out front and went home and looked it up in the phone book. John Wright, it said. Later on I learned John Wright owned a big foreign car repair and restoration shop and that's why he'd attended the car show, and that's when I decided to go to his shop and apply for a job. I figured it had to be in the stars, since the day I came in for my interview he said his head mechanic had just bought the farm a few weeks back and he was hard-up trying to find somebody to replace him. I told him I could do the job, and he said he'd give me the opportunity to prove it."

"I promised him I'd fix anything he put in front of me and I'd do a good job, but I didn't tell him what it was going to cost him in the end. I didn't mention one word about how I had it in my head that I was going to steal Teresa away from him as part of my take-home pay." I was pretty much out of my gourd when we started back down the road that night. I wasn't too talkative at that point, so I alternated between leaning back in my seat and listening to the radio and letting Sam talk uninterrupted about where he'd been all these years, what he'd been doing, how through all his lists of jobs and cheap apartments and sorry-ass towns the only constant he'd had the entire time was the Sunbeam, his Tiger, Ophelia, he called her. That's the name I finally gave her, he said, a testament to my old Shakespeare class and the fact that her family was extinct like mine and she was always in such a state where all she could do was sing songs and think about death like I did, but the fact was we were partners, and we were both of the mind that there just might be something coming one of these days for the two of us to stay alive for, new tires, new roads, restoration of our souls and spirits, rosemary for remembrance and pansies for thought, shit like that, finally perhaps for us to arrive at the glory we'd both glimpsed so long ago but had never managed to get close enough to touch.

Ophelia knew she was a fast car, one of a kind, and Sam thought much the same of himself. He was a notch above all the others, smarter, more appreciative of the stars in the sky and the glow of the moon, and he and Ophelia together traveled on, following their own star, until they had come to this stop in Nashville where a part of the puzzle was revealed to them. Here Sam could work at his new high-paying job and make enough to restore Ophelia to her former self, beauty and speed and in a class above the other cars in her path, keep her from the death and madness that was out in the world, and stay at this quest until Teresa Payne was his, this time for good, and then he and Teresa and Ophelia would drive away and travel down the road for as long as eternity happened to run.

Sam's tale reminded me of a song, and I leaned my head back against the window and looked out at the black highway going by.

I started humming a snatch of the tune under my breath. Inside my inebriated brain Tracy Chapman was singing "Fast Car." I could see all the words written on the road before us, and inside the Tiger Sam and I were together this night happy and dreaming and wishing that this moment we were living inside would hang around for the longest of whiles and our lives would never end, both of us hoping upon hope this would all go on forever and never stop, happy as hell there inside that fast car with a moon above us and the road straight ahead, praying and wishing and asking God to help Ophelia to still be fast enough for us to fly away.

Four

"I thought it was busy enough before, but I certainly wasn't prepared for the onslaught that came to the shop once Valentine's Day passed. The holiday, it seemed, was a symbol for the passing of winter and the coming of spring, and so the phone rang con- stantly and bright and shiny classic cars lined up at the doors to be looked over, repaired or added to, driven in by their owners or towed by trucks that circled the entrance to the shop from opening time and wrapped out into the street by noon. All the work areas and the waiting slots and the outside lot were filled with TR3s and MGTDs and Jags and Morgans and Auburns and more, and I even got issued on my own a Sprite and a Spitfire for oil changes and fluid checks. It wasn't much, these personal meager assignments, not in comparison with the super-expensive assignments the more experienced mechanics were given—especially Sam with a Bentley and two XKEs and a Lotus that looked like it had never seen the light of day—but just having the two cars parked in my section of the garage made me feel like I was now an actual member of the team, that I was finally qualified in my own right to tinker with these toys of the rich and powerful. I promised myself I'd do my best with the two cars, that I wouldn't do anything to screw them up and incur the wrath of the owners or my uncle on me, and if anything proved beyond my skillset I would go to Sam for advice and protection. Sam would be the guardian who would guide me through.

I used what I'd learned and looked at illustrations in manuals and watched YouTube videos on how to get tasks done, and I was able to finish with the Sprite and have it pass inspection the first time. There were two fellows, Tommy and Edgar, from Canada somewhere, who were like a team or something—maybe they were gay and lived together, I never found out—but when a car was completed by one of the mechanics it got passed on to Tommy and Edgar for a twenty-four-point check inspection, and the car had to pass one hundred percent before it was released back to its owner.

I found out pretty fast that this was one of the big selling points my uncle had instilled in his business from the onset. Customers from all over knew their car would be in one hundred percent working condition when they got it back, and by this maxim Wright's Foreign Car Repair's reputation grew and strengthened.

I was bound and determined my first two solo projects weren't going to get rejected by Tommy and Edgar and sent back for further work while the shame of a job not done to standard cast its cloud upon me, perhaps one done so badly it would never be lived down and I would never be trusted again, so when I started having problems with the Spitfire I spent a long time analyzing the engine and trying to figure out what was going on with it that I couldn't decipher. I'd done all that was supposed to be done when the car was brought in, but now when I turned the ignition it refused to run for no more than forty-five seconds before spewing and sighing and shaking and then completely dying out. After a half a day of trying to get it right, I finally picked up my phone and called Sam, who was up at the other end of the garage in his luxury compartment, reserved as it was for the top gun of the operation, and I asked him if he could come down and determine what the Spitfire was suffering from and if it might be fatal. I was getting nervous about it by then; I didn't want some dude's car to up and expire just all of a sudden when it had been okay until it was left in my care. I was six months at Wright's by then, doing okay and making more money than I ever had selling and distributing audio systems, going out some nights with the best-looking woman I'd ever managed to come close to, and I was trying my best not to screw anything up. I was about a thousand times better off than I'd been back in my Hannah Hills days, and I wanted to stay here in this place where there was a chance to breathe air that wasn't filled with failure and poverty.

The Spitfire's problem had something to do with the distributor and the timing, and Sam had it fixed in like three minutes, and it coasted through Tommy and Edgar and all their tests. Having two cars pass muster during a couple of days' work made me look good all around, and I never had to let on to anyone that if Sam hadn't come to my rescue I'd have been up the creek with no motor to get me back to the dock.

Sam never let on to anybody he'd come down and helped me. He was a good guy that way. Most people in the world would rub your nose in it then and later if you asked them for help, but not Sam. He let me take all the credit, however small it was. That was the way he was. He took care of me for some unknown reason.
I appreciated it and did my best to let him know how thankful I was we'd come to be pals.

• • • •

There was something about Jennifer Payne that kept me from wanting to be around her too awful much. I mean, I've already said how nice-looking she was and how she was looks-wise way above anybody else I'd ever had anything to do with, but the thing that held me back from going full-tilt with her was the fact that she simply didn't have much of a sense of humor. I'd say something in passing that was meant to be flippant or sarcastic in a light way, and she would always take it seriously, as if every word I said in jest was the deadly truth. It was like if I said I could just kill somebody for doing something, she would think I was on the brink of murder. If I said I'd done something a million times, she thought I had, that I was exhausted and on the verge of a complete physical collapse. I had to spend a lot of time explaining everything to her, telling her I didn't mean things the way she heard them, how I was kidding most of the time when she thought it was the absolute opposite way. After a while it got goddamned tiring. I grew buck-weary trying to make her understand a bunch of stuff that didn't matter in the first place. It got to where it didn't seem worth all the effort.
I knew it wasn't that she was stupid or anything. No, she was at least as smart as me and probably more so. It was simply the fact that she came from a place where no one ever had to crack jokes to keep from crying, no one had to paint the world a different color because the one they were born into had nothing of brightness and beauty within it. Jennifer Payne and I were from two different backgrounds, and there were times when the two simply didn't jive.

So instead of taking her out each and every night and blowing all my hard-earned dough on her fantastic features, sometimes I preferred staying in my room at my parents' house and watching movies on Turner Classics after taking a spin in the Civic knocking back a few tokes on a joint. No, I hadn't gone cold turkey on my vices. I still required weed every once in a while and a plethora of beer on those nights when Sam and I had one of our bull sessions, but it wasn't like I was doing anything to hurt anybody. I was only taking a few necessary steps to keep myself from going crazy. Unlike the doctrine Hannah Hills tried to instill in you, I knew I wasn't an addict or an alcoholic or anything negative like that. I was simply this dude in his late twenties trying to stay happy while he took in the hand life was dealing him. A fellow didn't want to get too happy or too sad before he had all his cards and could determine what to do with them. The bottom line was knowing how to stay in the game. Jennifer, being the great-looking woman she was, wasn't without possible suitors, and so after a couple of months we sort of drifted apart and I only saw her now and then, and thus was not kept abreast too much of what was going on in the shadows as far as Teresa and Sam were concerned. What I learned came from Sam himself, and since most of the time he was busy with Teresa he and I didn't spend as much time together as we had there for a while. I was kind of in the dark on what was going on, which I was soon to learn was probably a good place to be.

On a Thursday afternoon Sam came down to my workspace and asked me what I was doing on the coming Saturday. He wanted to know if I'd like to take a little jaunt with him to Memphis and cross the Mississippi and go to a car show outside Little Rock.

"It's mostly standard British cars," he said, "but this one is supposed to have several Sunbeams in it that I wouldn't mind taking a look at. Every blue moon or so I like to talk with other Tiger owners and see what they're doing with their cars to keep them ship-shape. There are times, of course, it gets a little depressing, because most of these dudes have a truckful of money and can do any damn thing they want, but it's still good for me to gather some new ideas and see if there's any way I can raise Ophelia up a grade or two, like maybe buy a new top or new seats for a good price or something like that. Generally, whatever I want to do I can't afford, but I'm at least keeping my eyes open in case I win the lottery or something like that and become suddenly rich and shitting gold doubloons. A show like this if nothing else gives me the opportunity to dream a little. I've also managed to save up a little money over the past couple of months, and it's burning a hole in my pocket. Maybe I'll break down and buy something."

As much as I admired Sam's Tiger, I still had reservations about driving three hundred miles back and forth in it on a day-long road trip, but Sam insisted the Sunbeam was in fine shape and hadn't let him down too many times before over the half-century he'd owned her. I wasn't exactly wooed by his description of the car only breaking down not "too many times before" in the past, and would have preferred if he had lied and said such misfortunes had never happened at all. I thought back to my days as a Midget owner and remembered the number of times I'd been stranded in strange places, in deserted parking lots or on highways or in the middle of nose-to-nose traffic, and there was a part of me that wanted to spend my Saturday in my safe little room watching whatever movie Turner Classics was serving up that day and staying nice and calm and cozy. But Sam was persistent in clinging to driving the Tiger to Arkansas (I suppose the idea of taking an adventure in an aging Honda Civic didn't appeal to his sense of adventure much) and so I drove to his duplex early Saturday morning and parked on the side he rented and knocked on the door, hoping he'd overslept and we'd decide to cancel the trip.

But he was awake. He was up and at them. He'd already ventured down to a Krispy Kreme and bought a dozen doughnuts, and handed me a plate with two glazed on it and a cup of coffee, black, the only way he drank it and the way he thought the rest of the world ought to take it too.

"Wolf those down and wipe your face and let's hit the road. If we get our asses in gear we can be there in three hours."

I did as I was told, deducing and configuring in my mind how if we were going to arrive at our destination in three hours we would have to average in the neighborhood of ninety miles an hour to do it, which I wasn't that revved up to experience.

"We can be late," I said. "I really don't mind. If it comes

down to an hour of looking at foreign cars or dying I'll give up punctuality every time."

"That's what's wrong with you, Leonard. You never want to challenge yourself."

The Tiger shook and rattled and shimmied all the way down 40 West. Several times I heard noises within the frame that sounded like the car was preparing to fall apart, and there was a groaning clamor coming through the dash that made me think some demon from Hell was fixing to burst through and go for my throat. It was hot and I kept smelling oil and smoke, but at last we came into Memphis and crossed the bridge and despite all my previous fears, there we were in Arkansas. Twenty-five minutes later we turned off at an exit and I saw the signs for the car show a half mile away. All the way down, above the sound of the Tiger's V-8 and its growls and grunts and heavy breathing, Sam talked about when he first was able to legally get the Sunbeam on the road.

"The first date I had in Ophelia was with this chick who was the head majorette in my high school's band. I played football and basketball back then, and though none of our athletic teams were ever worth a shit, the band was like this big award-winning combine. They were always winning awards and marching in the Christmas Parade downtown or going off to California or Hawaii to strut their stuff, and Janet Hamblin—that was her name—was the girl out front by the drum major who twirled and squatted and threw herself up in the air while the rest of the majorettes stood around and watched and held their batons at attention until it was time to start marching again. They'd follow her out and twirl a few times and join in with the band and spell out letters in the middle of the football field or at half court or at an intersection that had been roped off for the occasion. Janet, though, was the one everybody took particular notice of. She had legs that went all the way up to her ass, and she could bend and contort in just about every position you could imagine. And believe me, I imagined a lot back then. I dated her for about six weeks straight when I first got Ophelia on the road, and I was bound and determined I was going to figure out a way to screw her in the front seat of the car one way or another. I don't know why it was so much of an obsession for me to do such a thing, but I guess I'd spent so many adolescent hours sitting in the driver's seat of the Sunbeam unable to go anywhere and fantasizing about girls and their bodies and all that it felt like I owed it to the car for allowing me to sit there and dream about everything for so many years. I figured it was me and Ophelia together even from the very first, and so I thought we ought to be together the first time I got lucky with some girl."

"Did you and the fair Janet ever consummate your relationship?"

"Hell, no. She was one of those good girls who went to church on Sunday and was saving herself for her future husband, who we both knew wasn't going to be me. Besides, she was always scared shitless of the Sunbeam. She was a nervous wreck every time we went to a movie or anywhere because I tended to drive fast. There wasn't any damn way I was going to get to take advantage of her inside the Tiger, since Janet considered it to be nothing but a deathtrap. You may want to die in this car, she told me, but I don't. I plan on living to a ripe old age. I remember her saying that a couple of thousand times. She probably did live to be an old buzzard too. I hate thinking about that kind of stuff these days—it plays on my mind. All these pretty girls that made your blood rush back when you were in the first throes of being a man, and then you blink your eyes and the whole world's turned into a rest home all at once. These days all the pretty girls are getting around in walkers or wheelchairs, they're all stooped over and wrinkled and everything of them that used to be firm and high has gone south. You look them in the eye and you don't know who they are, and if you do, they don't remember the first thing about you because their minds have all flown away to be with Jesus."

"Boy," I said, "listening to you go on this way makes me never want to get any older. I mean, I'm miserable enough already. Maybe I should just save myself from suffering and go jump off a bridge somewhere. Why don't you stop when we get to the Mississippi and let me out?"

"Getting old isn't so bad," Sam said. "It's watching everything around you do the same is what's so awful."

We spent most of the morning hiking around the field where

the show was being held. I already knew how Sam was an authority on cars and how they ran, their differences and similarities and all that, but I was still amazed at how he knew the histories of carmakers and when something came out and when some model went out of existence and why it all went down the way it did. Before we sat down for lunch I knew about why Triumph folded and when the last MG rolled out the factory door at Abington and what BMW stood for (in English, Bavarian Motor Works) and, something he was really an expert on, how the Sunbeam Alpine evolved into becoming the Sunbeam Tiger. I heard so much about compression and frames and performance engines and cubic inches that I couldn't keep up, my head was spinning, and I felt like a dumbass taking in all this information that I knew I'd never retain. I knew I would never be a master mechanic like Sam or some of the others at the shop. It simply wasn't in me. I couldn't be counted on to perform any acts of sweeping majesty or bring some classic automobile back from the dead. I was only good for a few simple procedures, changing oil, adjusting this and that, turning a screw, but that was it. I could barely be trusted to get behind the wheel and drive someone's car into a stall to be repaired by somebody other than me who had the first inkling of sense.

"You're not so bad," Sam said. "I've watched you. You're no worse than anybody else who's just starting out. You have to remember that most automobile repairs have nothing to do with rocket science—it's A, B, C, one, two, three. All the average person has to do is follow the instructions. It's like a doctor telling you to take two aspirins and go to bed, but in the case a real killer of a malady comes along, well, that's when you have to call in a specialist. That's what I am. That's the way I got to be sitting out in my car as a kid and reading everything I could come across, looking at stuff all the time and figuring out why it's there and how it works, and then later when I could get around and go places I'd stop by shops and talk to mechanics and look things up in the library and order books in the mail after I got a job and had some spending money. I made somewhat of a choice, see? I played a little sports and dated a few girls, but most of the time I fell out of the social scene and worked so I could go to school and get out of town. Paris, Tennessee, home of the world's biggest fish fry—that's where I came from. Not that it was terrible, but if you've got half a brain you know there's got to be more to life than that. My mom wasn't going to ever be able to afford sending me to school and financing my getaway, so I knew I had to do it myself. And I was right. She died my freshman year, broke and swimming in medical bills, and it was up to me to settle everything and start making my way alone. And I did pretty good, buddy, I did pretty good for a while. Maybe not everything was down the road legal, but I got along okay until the shit hit the fan and I was invited to spend some time behind bars for being a goddamn menace to society."

We'd just finished looking at the Sunbeam section of the show for the third time. There were three Sunbeams displayed, two Tigers and an Alpine. All of them were red. They were shiny with gleaming bumpers and spotless interiors with bucket seats and lustrous steering wheels. Their hoods were raised to expose clean and sparkly engines, new belts, polished crankcases, everything Sam's Ophelia did not possess. I saw him inspect each car and detected a slight smile on his face, as if he was glad to see that with all these perfections on these cars he still preferred his Ophelia. In the end these Sunbeams would be loaded up on a trailer and carried back to where they resided in spotless garages and clean concrete, but that was okay with Sam, because in an hour or so he would be headed back up 40 East to cross the river and buzz home driving his own Sunbeam Tiger back to Nashville.

· · · ·

For some strange reason I'm still not able to completely understand, from that time on after that Saturday trip with Sam my passion for Jennifer began to slip even more. It wasn't that my physical side didn't appreciate looking at her when she came near or feeling the softness of her skin on mine, but it was like there was this sudden loss of urgency in my pursuit of her in the wholeness sense. It was like the time would come—not all the time, sometimes not for a week or so in-between—when I would all at once be tired of listening to her and not much care to try and kiss her or make an effort for my body to be joined with hers. It wasn't glaringly evident--even I didn't notice the change right-off--but the idea and sense of the reduction of fire and imaginative conception of the two of us as a couple gradually began appearing in my consciousness. It was a strange concept to be sure, the idea that I was turning away from such a marvelous creature as Jennifer Payne, because I was, after all, abiding in my late twenties, and a dreamboat like Jennifer was what I had been pursuing all my life.

It was one night during this changing of my emotional guard that Jennifer and I sat on her back patio on a Memorial Day evening. We'd both had the day off and I'd made a date with her to go to dinner and a movie (some Harry Potter flick I can't remember the actual title of), and now we occupied a rocker/divan in her small space outdoors, which consisted of a table and four chairs, the divan, a small grill where maybe four hamburgers could be cooked simultaneously, and a wooden privacy fence to separate the neighbors and keep from having to gaze at parked cars.

Somehow, as it always seemed to, the conversation had turned to Teresa and Sam and Teresa's and John's failing marriage and if Teresa and my uncle would ever get to the point where they called it quits. It was a never-ending gossipy scandal that neither one of us could stop thinking about for more than a few minutes at a time.

"I don't see why they shouldn't," I said. "It's not like either one of them is happy with the other. Is there anything they have in common? Whatever it is they like to do they always make sure they do it apart. The only time they're together is when he needs her to attend a banquet or some society gig with him, or if they need to be photographed by some church or the city while they're performing a grand charitable act so they can later both be lauded and praised as emissaries from Heaven or something."

"That's exactly why they stay together," Jennifer said. "They need each other for precisely those things, and as long as they get rewarded for being pillars of the community they aren't going to do anything different. All will be well as long as nobody does anything shocking or seamy publicly where the world might catch a glimpse that all isn't up to snuff in Paradise."

"It's a crappy way to live, if you ask me."

"Oh, they're used to it. I don't know how your uncle feels about it, but I do know Aunt Teresa considers her lifestyle these days to be a jillion times better than it was when she was growing up. Back then my mother and her were close to being poor. Not dirt poor, mind you, but certainly not well-off enough to have their own cars or go to private schools or have closets overflowing with fancy clothes. Aunt Teresa paid my way through school, but it wasn't that way with her or mom when they were my age. They had none of that. If the two of them hadn't gotten financial assistance neither one would have been able to go to college or anything."

"Teresa got a scholarship?"

"You bet she did. Academic. She's always been smart as a whip, much more than anybody else in the family. Mother got in because she played basketball and was pretty good until she got pregnant with my brother. Me, I had to study my behind off the entire four years until I graduated, but everything always came easy to Aunt Teresa. She was way ahead of everybody. She knew everything and always had everything figured out when everybody else was sitting there stumped."

"Funny she acts this way with Sam. You'd think she'd be wise enough to keep her distance from one of her husband's employees. She ought to know nothing good is ever going to come of it." "Sam Thornton is different. She always says that. She can't figure out what to do with him, and that's the first time I can ever remember anything stumping her like that."

There was something about the way she talked about Teresa that night that gave me a moment of pause, that made me want to say goodnight and go home and get in bed by myself, because all of a sudden none of what the world had to offer was making a whole lot of sense to me, Teresa and Sam and what they'd done in the past and what they were doing now, or Jennifer and the way her hair became stringy and her eyes colored over black from the eyeliner and the fake eyelashes on those occasions when we made love, and how there was generally nothing for us to talk about when we were through, and me working for my uncle who wasn't near the man I thought he was, who was nothing like my dad but was rich enough to separate me from the sorry circumstances I'd placed myself in all my life if only I'd live the life he was offering me and stay in my place, and me sleeping in my high school bed a decade later but somehow no older or wiser, not removed much at all from that kid who'd wondered what it was all about and if he'd ever get lucky enough to escape the meaningless sea he dove into each day. I drove home that night in the Civic and wondered if things would be different if the Civic was a Jaguar instead, or if I would still feel the same and be the same no matter what model automobile I was driving, but this time be disguised behind the wheel as a young man of the world who has found success in the world.

When I got in bed it was too damn quiet in the house, so I turned on the television and watched the last forty-five minutes of "The Adventures of Robin Hood," wishing like hell I was Errol Flynn instead of my own sorry self, and knowing if I was old handsome Errol I'd have not a damn thing to worry about anymore.

Five

In the first weeks after Memorial Day the temperature hovered in the lower sixties during the day, hardly the kind of weather conducive for swimming and sunning and other summertime activities. Sometimes Sam and I would go to watch the minor league baseball team play, on those occasions when Teresa was busy with her clubs or charities or had to be gathered with the elite ruling class somewhere for a dinner or a benefit at a time when people like that wished to congregate and breathe the air most regular folks never were provided the opportunity to sample. More times than not I'd have to remember to wear a jacket to the games during that coolish time so I wouldn't freeze before the seventh inning stretch, and even when donning what clothing I thought would be appropriate it still proved not enough to keep me from having the shivers during the games. Drinking cold beer didn't help either, and I finally had to settle for cups of hot coffee every two innings or so, which forced me into the restrooms for frequent urination, at which time I'd miss parts of the game. I couldn't win.

By this time my relationship with Jennifer had receded to truly low ebb, and I knew these failings at a romantic relationship were all my doing. I honestly believed that if I had only stuck to the path and acted like a good suitor with her, held doors and provided dinner and feigned interest when she began recounting the rigors of being a spokeswoman for a luxury automobile dealership that I could have secured a place in her affections and achieved the role of Significant Other, but, like I mentioned, there was just something lacking in our chemistry that kept me from wading in and getting wet all over. I could get damp from time to time, sure, but maybe it was because I knew, whether anyone else did or not, that I was an imposter in this current swell of progress I was engaged in, and that in only a little while the world would find me out. This would include Jennifer herself, and I had an abiding dread she would cast me out when the truth came to the fore for my being incapable and not up to standards in the end, and such an action might just come about publicly, which with my low self-esteem I would not be able to stand. It's one thing to know you don't measure up; it's another thing completely for the rest of the world to be aware of what a failure you are too.

Sam and I were walking out of the stadium after a game to the Sunbeam to head home when we came upon the sight of a couple of kids—one inside, one out—going through the Tiger's trunk and interior. They hadn't had to break in to get at what was inside since Sam didn't believe in locking the doors of a convertible (all that does is tell somebody to slash a hole in the top with a knife, he said, and then there you are having to get yourself a new top, which ain't cheap, which costs a pretty damn penny these days) and so all they'd had to do was open the door and get in. The trunk was sprung, probably by a crowbar, and it stood open while a fellow leaned over going through it seeing what he could find. Both wore hoodies covering their heads, but I could tell they were kids. I still didn't want to have anything to do with them, since one thing you learn when you're living inside the Naked Frigging City is that a lot of kids have guns and aren't the least bit afraid to use them.

Sam, though, was having none of this. He left me standing by myself being cautious and ran toward the Tiger like he was playing fullback for the Titans, and had not the kid inside the car seen him coming from twenty yards away he would have been pinned within the Tiger and dragged out for the beating of his life, gun or no gun. At that moment Sam Thornton looked pretty much invulnerable to me, like a bullet or a blade would never be enough to pierce his core.

The kid jumped out of the car and yelled at his partner, and instead of standing and the two of them taking on this old man barreling toward them, they both ran off as fast as their Nikes could take them. I thought it would be a brave gesture to move from my spot and catch up with Sam if I could, to maybe at least try and act like I was going to go into battle with him as his comrade, but by the time I made it to him at the car the two kids were long gone and he was already busy examining Ophelia for possible damage. The glove compartment was open and some papers and spare napkins were spilled out on the floorboard, the ignition starter was dangling with wires exposed, probably as a preamble to getting hot-wired, and a spare jacket lay on the ground by the trunk, the only thing that had been in there to begin with. To my way of thinking, this didn't seem like too much of a tragedy. It was a minor violation of Sam's property, but I learned something right then about Sam that I haven't forgotten since.

"I've busted my ass trying to keep this car as original as possible," he explained. He was busy rubbing at a scratch by the trunk latch, trying to determine if the scratch had come from what had been used to break in. "I haven't broadcasted this much to anyone because I figured it would get back to your uncle, but I've been staying over at work a lot lately working on Ophelia, fixing stuff that's way overdue and getting it back to prime again. God knows she's never been prime as long as I've owned her, but I've never had the opportunity or resources to get the necessary work done all these years either. It's been a long time, and it's hard to believe this car is so tough it's weathered not getting tender loving care during all that period. What I've been doing is after we close for the day I stick around and work on stuff up into the night—been doing it almost a month now, and in another week she'll be ready for some body work and a new paint job."

"You should have let me know. I'd have stayed and helped you."

"I didn't want you to get involved. The thing of it is I've had to use some of the shop's inventory to get things the way I want mechanically. I've put in a new clutch and replaced the brakes and had a bunch of stuff shipped here to me that I couldn't afford right now, so I thought it was best to do it on the sly in case anything came to light and your uncle thought I was stealing things. No, I've got a list of what I've done and I'm going to make a bill out of it and pay for it all when I'm done. I started to ask him if he'd mind if I did such a thing but I was afraid he'd say no. I have the feeling he doesn't trust too many people in the world. If he found out you were in this with me he'd probably fire you too."

"Why is there all of a sudden such a hurry? After all, the Sunbeam's been this way for years. Why the big rush now?"

"Get in and I'll explain it to you."

As we drove along he told me more about him and the Tiger and their history together, and how the Sunbeam was a part of his plan of regaining Teresa Payne-Wright for good.

"See, Leonard, I told you Teresa didn't even know me that first night we met her and Jennifer. I was just some stranger who worked for her husband, hanging out with her husband's nephew who she didn't really know either. It took until later when she saw the Tiger that it finally came to her who I was. It was because she remembered the car. She'd ridden in Ophelia that one night when we were together, and she remembered having seen it around school a time or two before that. It all came back to her then. It was thirty years later, but it all came back in a rush."

"I guess Ophelia's not an easy car to forget."

"No, she's not. But what got to me was when Teresa laughed and said I'd kept it exactly the way it was back then, that nothing had changed. She laughed and said it still needed a coat of paint and how she hoped I wouldn't hit a bump and the floorboard would fall through. I didn't say anything back, just sort of went along with it, you know? But it hit a nerve in me somewhere, even more than the initial shock of being astounded from the fact that I'd run into Teresa again. I already knew from the first time I spotted her at the car show I'd somehow find a way to see her again on a regular basis, and suddenly after years of scraping by and moving around and trying to find some place to fit into I had the distinct feeling I was going to get back into the world by doing my best and looking my best, and since Ophelia was a dominant part of who I was and what I did, I resolved I was going to do the same for her too. She'd be a brand-new car before I was finished."

Suddenly Sam punched the accelerator and the car jumped and my head flew back against the seat. He shifted from second to third and for a moment it was like we'd been shot from a Barnum and Bailey cannon, and when he settled into fourth gear we were cruising along at an easy eighty-five on the interstate, the exit ramps and the illuminated signs whizzing by too fast to read or take. Then he gradually slowed and we hummed along at the speed limit.

"I have to watch it, I don't need another ticket," he said. "I forget sometimes. I've had more than my share over the years already."

He adjusted his grip on the wheel and looked out the window.

"Any time I see Teresa now she insists on driving wherever we go. 'I don't trust that car of yours,' she always says. 'It's either going to fall apart one of these days going down the road or I'm going to catch some deathly disease just by sitting in it. There's bound to be some poisonous germ somewhere inside it from staying decrepit for so many years.' Then she laughs and says I can drive whenever I decide to get a new car. It's all a big joke to her." We pulled into his drive and I got out and loaded up in the Civic to go home. When I drove off Sam was still outside looking Ophelia over, making sure she hadn't been mortally wounded during the evening's fray.

. . . .

I had a habit at the time of leaving my cellphone in the car whenever I went anyplace, mainly because it had become a form of leash on me as far as my parents were concerned. I couldn't really get angry at them for being so possessive and inquiring of my whereabouts all the time, simply because I hadn't exactly instilled in them any kind of confidence in the way I went about my daily dealings with life, seeing how they'd had to foot the bill on my stay at Hannah Hills and advance me the money to pay back my former employer as part of my plea bargain with the stipulation I was going to pay them back later when I got settled into my new respectable life working at a decent job and becoming a first-class citizen once more. I guessed because of this I owed them the decency to let them know where I was going when I left the house and, because I was living under their roof, when I might return, but I got to where there was rebellion still brewing in me from my days as a teenager under their tutelage and I looked for ways to free myself from whatever small bondages they held me under.

I'd lock my cellphone in the car, or purposely leave it on my dresser at home so I couldn't be contacted while I was going to dinner with Jennifer or going to bed with her those times when I could summon up the physical passion and didn't waste the majority of time considering how under her makeup she maybe wasn't as pretty as I'd first thought or not as smart and maybe, indeed, was a little on the shallow side that no one in the world knew about but me, certainly not those millions of eyes who saw her selling Mercedes Benzes and Range Rovers and Cadillacs on TV and wondered what she looked like naked, and I didn't want my folks calling wanting a little chat while I was flopping around with her, or if I was drinking beer with Sam or gone off on any number of excursions with him as Ben Jonson and me as Boswell attempting to memorize and observe each tale he imparted my way. I guess it wasn't entirely honorable shirking my parents like that, since they'd been practically the only ones who'd covered my ass back when I'd bared it to the world for a good shellacking, but I was coming up on the end of my twenties and the dreaded onset of my thirties and getting closer to that point in time where I could never be trusted again by myself or anybody, and the thought of still being under my parents' thumbs at that stage of my life didn't set right in my head. I had to show a little independence one way or another.

That night I'd gone out by myself and ate at a Burger King and smoked a joint and driven around listening to the Classic Rock radio station for a couple of hours. I hadn't even checked to see if I had any messages on my phone to read, but was taking a meandering passage driving home when I heard it buzzing while I sat at a red light. I started to let it ring and go into a message, but then I thought how perhaps it might be Jennifer and that maybe I could go over to her place now instead of going home, being right then in one of my reoccurring states of horniness as I was prone to at times and wanting to engage in lascivious acts instead of seeing what was on Turner Classics when I got home. I reached and retrieved the phone and saw it was my mother calling and started to let it go, but for some reason I answered it. I guess I was curious. It was eleven o'clock and I'd never known either of my folks to try and call me that late in the evening. They were always asleep.

"Where are you?" my mother said. "I need you to come home.

Something terrible has happened."

"What's wrong?"

"Your father has had a stroke," she said. "I don't know an easy way to tell you this, Leonard, but he's dead. He died sitting in his chair in the living room right after dinner. He was reading a National Geographic and it just fell out of his hands and his arm dropped and his head fell over. For a minute I thought he'd fallen asleep, but it was too fast. I knew no one went to sleep that quickly. I knew something was wrong."

"Where are you now?"

"I'm at home. There are people here, paramedics, the police, a couple of others. I'm having to answer questions and call people to let them know. I've been trying to find you for hours now."

"I left my phone in the car."

I didn't tell her how I do such things as that accidentally on purpose.

There was a big part of me that wanted to take my time getting home. I didn't know quite what to expect when I got there, but I had an idea there would be a preacher and some family friends and probably some relations, my mother's side mostly, since there wasn't much on my father's side except two aunts who lived out of state and Uncle John, who was here in town but who I doubted could be reached this time of the evening, especially if he was out carousing with other women as I'd been told he did on a regular basis. I wondered if I was going to have to be the one to drive in to the shop in the morning and tell him his little brother was dead. I realized I was allowing myself to let life play out in my head again, that I was avoiding the reality of my father's demise, and that I ought to hurry and get home and start facing up to it. Everything else would take care of itself.

I wasn't too far wrong in all my imaginings, because there was my parents' preacher on the scene and my aunts had been alerted and were making plans to come in, and Uncle John had been contacted too and was seated in a chair in the living room by himself when I came in. He was alone. Teresa wasn't with him, and I wondered where she might possibly be.

"Here you are," Uncle John stated.

"Yes. I just found out. I came as fast as I could."

"This was very sudden," he said. "Your father hasn't even been sick lately. He was feeling fine the last time I talked to him. When your mother called and said what had happened it was hard for me to believe it. I guess because I'm the oldest one in the family I've always believed I'd be the first to go. I thought all my sisters and your dad would outlive me."

"Daddy was sixty-two," I said. I thought about it for a minute. It seemed like a big number, but then it seemed small too. It seemed like he was an old man who was too young to die. "This is going to take a while to sink in," I said. "It's a little too much." I paused a heartbeat or two. I didn't want to talk to Uncle John anymore. "I better go in and find Mother."

I left him alone in the living room and walked back into the house looking for my mother. She was in the kitchen with the preacher and a neighbor who'd come by. When she saw me she started to cry. I didn't cry at all. I just let her hug me and sob on my shoulder and tell me what a good man my dad had been, how it was going to be hard to learn to live without him. I didn't say anything since I'd been living without him and her in a way for a while now already. It wasn't that I didn't see them, because I did every day. It was just that I wasn't really there all that time like they thought I was, I was gone off somewhere in my mind, and I wondered if either my dad or her had ever figured that out. It was hard to tell. All I really knew was that they didn't really know me, which was sort of a shame after all this time. I guess I should have felt sorrier than I did, since the fact that we were nothing but strangers was mostly my fault.

In the next week that followed, through the arrangements and the ceremonies and the burial, I was surrounded by people but mostly kept to myself. Jennifer attended the funeral with Teresa, the two of them coming in a separate car from Uncle John. Sam came to both the visitation and the funeral and stayed away from the crowd, not talking to Teresa or Uncle John or anyone but me for a few seconds. I wondered what was going on between all these people, what it was they were up to that they shouldn't be doing, how among them I was now fatherless in the world and how it felt strangely not too much different than before, that death didn't seem to have much to do with what was going on here on earth with all these other living beings around me, who were still all out there on their big stage speaking their lines and playing their parts, looking for their portion of the spotlight.

. . . .

On a night following my father's funeral I lay in bed for a time watching Gene Kelly lament over the loss of Leslie Caron by going into a ballet fantasy with legions of dancers leaping about him, and I knew if I watched long enough Leslie would return from that portion of the world where Gene thought she had been lost forever and the two would be reunited and Paris and the world would be at their feet from then forward. How nice that must be, I thought as I dozed off, getting everything you wish for and never having to worry about doing without it ever again.

As I pondered the world in my dreamlike state, I saw the window open and a beautiful woman in a white gown appeared. At the time I thought she was Lana Turner, but I'm not sure now. Maybe I was getting her mixed up with somebody else. Still, it might have been Lana, of whom I have always held a certain affinity. The woman asked if I was feeling better now, if I had learned how to get over my state of guilt about the death of my father, if I knew that it wasn't really my fault that he and I (and my mother too) never had the sort of relationship one saw on the screen, like Judge Hardy and Andy and his family, like all the other fathers and sons and families I'd grown up watching and believing in while being spoon-fed with the idea that all this family affection and respect was the way it was in every corner of the world. But it's not, the Lana Turner figure said. You can forget all that. What is really true is you can have whatever you want and all you have to do is ask the moon and stars and it will be given to you. It can happen, Leonard, even to you. Do you want Jennifer Payne? You can have her. Do you want to rise up in your new occupation and become the lucky person your uncle gives the keys to the kingdom to when he retires? When he expires? He'll die, Leonard, just like your father did, just like people die every day. Say the word to your Hollywood dream in the sky and you can have all that until your day for checking out comes too. Would you like that? And would you like to have me too? Me, who could be Lana Turner if you please and you could have the entire world with the most beautiful woman in the galaxy topping it off like a big red cherry on an endless milkshake?

I saw myself then being rewarded with all I'd ever dreamed of, money and Lana Turner and fast cars and pleasure domes wherein to abide. I heard music and saw beautiful sunrises and breathtaking sunsets. I traveled through a kaleidoscope of cities and countries, canyons and mountains, balconies and beaches, and I ordered drinks and food from never-ceasing menus set before me, waiters who politely answered yes to my orders, the populations of towns and municipalities nodding agreement to my wishes, and with each measure of assent and triumph I felt something grow inside me burning and becoming larger all the time. My Lana Turner visitor was laughing at me then, but now she wasn't Lana of The Bad and the Beautiful or The Postman Always Rings Twice or The Three Musketeers, but was older suddenly this night and aged and it was hard to see who she'd once been those many decades ago. She stood before me shriveled and haggard, wrinkled and defeated by time, and she never had to say anything else, she didn't have to let me know how having everything sometimes didn't work out in the end game, that when you have it you have to hold on with both hands and all your fingers or it will sure as shooting slip away when you reach for something else, and how sad it is to watch it go after you thought you had it for good, or worse, how you might finally have it and then just like that want it to leave you and disappear like it had never been there to begin with, but that was the way it was, when you had it for a while and maybe for good and you find it hadn't been what you'd been dreaming of in the beginning, it was different and it made you different too, and so it was you were both there together and yet you were both in the end gone away from each other too.

Then my Lana Turner left me and I was more than glad to wake up.

Six

It was July before I knew it. In the weeks since my dad's death I'd done my best to be the dutiful son and be around for my mother in case she needed me. This turned out to be a big mistake on my part, because spending more time with my mother only reinforced the belief in my mind that I'd somehow been adopted from an early age and had no inherited similarities with her at all. We didn't like the same foods, she tucked her nose up at my choices of reading material, and she never could understand my propensity for old movies that didn't have a happy ending. It had been that way from the very beginning with us, with me not wanting to go to church or join the Royal Ambassadors or go on vacation with her and my father after I reached the age of twelve. I guess if I'd just ran out in the road after Sunday School when I was about nine and got squashed by a Mack truck our relationship might have been saved. She would have had happy memories and known in her heart I was gone to Heaven to be with Jesus, but me making it through adolescence and growing up to be someone always trying to go against the Will of the Creator was just too much for her, and so it was all downhill between the two of us from that time on, and the past weeks spent in close proximity with each other only reinforced that fact.

I saw very little of Jennifer by then, which was my fault entirely, but I still carried around my usual cross for self-crucifixion when it came to relationships with women. Even though I was the one who always distanced myself from any entanglements, it was still somebody else's fault that I had to suffer in the end, because it had been prophesized to me from an early age that girls and women and females in general were eternally going to make me miserable in the long run. They weren't going to like me much. They were going to make me say things I didn't mean and go places where I wasn't wanted and attempt feats that were not in my capabilities and always end up failing and wondering why I'd bothered to live through such travails, since the chances were good bad scenes with women were almost certain to happen again so why not go ahead and be done with it. By making sure I was out of striking distance from Jennifer, I gave myself a sense of security that perhaps when radioactivity from her essence began drifting my way—as I knew it inevitably would--I would have ample time to construct a bomb shelter and get myself safely hidden inside it before her poison took me to either the grave or a form of living hell I'd be better off dead than having to inhabit for even the shortest period of time.

So, it came to a shock to me in the early hours of July 5 when my cell began buzzing on my bedstand, gyrating around in a circle like it was teaming with electronic snakes, and I opened one eye and watched it dancing there like it was possessed, stared at it and wished it to quit, and when it didn't I knew I would have to answer it. I couldn't just lay there and go back to sleep, because that was over now and I was teaming with curiosity and wonder and knowing also that I'd feel guilty later if I hadn't answered when something dire and important had required my attention.

It was Jennifer on the other end. I couldn't tell if she was happy or sad, but I did know she'd been drinking and probably doing something else on top of that, because she was out of breath one minute and then alternately giggling and crying the other. I could already determine this wasn't simply a social call.

"I hope I didn't wake you up," she stated. "I was hoping you were watching television like you say you do so much, and then I wouldn't have to feel so bad about spoiling your beauty sleep."

"Too late for that now, but since I'm never going to make it to being classified in the beautiful category it doesn't make that much difference. I wasn't expecting to hear from you in the middle of the night though, so I guess this is a surprise. I hope nothing's wrong to make you call me like this."

"Well, there is a little something gumming up the works, Leonard, I might as well be honest about it. See, I seem to be in a ditch and I can't get out. I think I need a little help." "You're in a ditch? You mean with your car?"

"Yes," she tittered, "you have it right. Somehow me and my vehicle have wound up in somebody's ditch. There's a fence and a mailbox here, and my car is way down in a gully beside them."

This seemed funny to her, so she started laughing again. Finally she stopped and said, "I guess I'm calling because I need a little help."

"Are you hurt?"

"Only a bump on my head. Other than that, just my pride. But my car may be dead. It just won't move."

"Where are you?"

"That's what's so funny. I'm down the road from your house, a couple of driveways away. I guess I was stalking you and didn't keep my eyes on the road."

"I'll be there in a minute."

The good thing was I didn't have to be at work in the morning—Uncle John had closed the shop on the fifth so everyone could enjoy Independence Day without having to wake up the next day with a hangover and then having to come to work—but I still wasn't crazy about sneaking out the door in the wee small hours and tiptoeing down the street in search of a drunken girl with her car in my neighbors' ditch, no matter how good-looking the drunken girl was. I wondered how in god's name I was going to pull her car out of the ditch and get her out of there before somebody called the police. I concluded that the prospects were pretty damn zilch for me to accomplish such a feat.

Jennifer had somehow managed to dislodge herself from the car in the ditch and was standing on the road under a streetlight looking at her phone. I wasn't sure if she was calling her car dealership to come and get her car out of its resting spot or if she was dialing AAA to see about a tow, but the fact that she was standing up and not helpless in the car made me feel a lot less like Sir Galahad than I'd wanted to be. It was one thing to pull me out of a deep beer-aided sleep on a morning I'd planned on sleeping in, but she could have at least been trapped and helpless while I came to her aid—maybe if it had been that way I might at least have been deserving of some sort of sexual favor for my heroic actions later on. But the truth was Jennifer was capable of movement without me, and I was probably just another in a long line of contacts she would be calling to help her escape from this unpleasant situation that somehow had just happened along.

"Here you are," she said brightly.

"Yeah, and here you are," I told her, trying to put some severity into my manner the way I'd always seen grownups do before as I was growing up. She just smiled at my huffiness, so I knew I wasn't doing a very good job showing my displeasure.

But, then again, Jennifer was one pretty girl, even if she was out here in the middle of the night three sheets to the wind with her Mercedes convertible in a ditch, and I have already expostulated the way I am when dealing with attractive females, so I guess my true feelings were showing through despite my better intentions. "I guess you can see I've got a little problem here," she said. She watched me walk along the rim of the ditch inspecting the damage. There was a nice crease in her driver's side panel that I could see, but because of the angle I couldn't tell how bad the passenger side was. I did notice the flattened mailbox joined to the front frame of the car, and it looked in lots worse shape than the Mercedes, which made me think back on Jennifer's commercials and how she talked about how safe all the Mercedes and Cadillacs and Range Rovers her company sold were compared to everything else on the road. Maybe she was right, but it was a hell of a time for me to find out it was true. I would have preferred listening to the sales pitch on television.

"Ain't no way you're going to be able to drive this out of here," I said. "We're going to have to call a wrecker."

"I've already called my work. They're sending one out right away to get it." She smiled again and wiggled her nose like she was Samantha Stevens and all the problems would be solved in a jiffy. "It's not my car, you know. It's a company car I get to drive as part of my employment package. I can have another one in the morning when I come in. I think I'll get a Cadillac this time."

A light from the front porch came on and the door opened. It looked like every room in the house was lit up. This wasn't good. More than ever I didn't want to be here. I wanted to be back home in my bed.

"There's fixing to be trouble. The cops are bound to be here any minute."

"I've called Aunt Teresa already too. She's getting John to

make some calls and get a few people down here to help."

"You don't seem to understand, Jennifer. You're intoxicated. They'll make you blow into a machine and then they'll arrest you. It's called Driving Under the Influence. I'm pretty damn sure you won't pass the test." "You worry too much, Leonard. I don't think it will come to that. It is, after all, just a little accident. Accidents happen all the time."

She was out there all right, high and hopped with bubbles coming out of her ears, so I knew any more lecturing I had to do was not going to be heard. I was trying to think of a way to whisk her out of there when two police cruisers pulled up with their blue lights flashing and a couple of high-beam spotlights on the two of us, like we were Fred and Ginger getting ready to do the Continental, and I knew the best thing I could do from there on out was stand still and speak when spoken to and when they said jump politely ask how high.

I have never liked cops. I didn't want to be one when I was a kid and I never have liked seeing one anywhere in the vicinity of anything shady I was doing, not that I'm guilty of many high crimes or anything like that—just the one that sent me to Hannah Hills, but that had been a doozy.

"Is this your car?" one of the officers said to me.

"No, sir. I'm not driving. I just live down the street."

He shone his flashlight in my eyes to see if I was lying. Any minute I expected to be tasered.

"If you live down the street how come you're not home in bed?" He shone the light on Jennifer, let it linger a lot longer than he had on me, which convinced me he was busy taking in the scenery.

"Is this your car, ma'am?"

"Not exactly," Jennifer said. "It belongs to my company. I just get to drive it because I do commercials for them."

"You look familiar," the second cop said. "Have I seen you on TV or something?"

"That's a very good possibility," she smiled. "Mercedes and Range Rovers and Cadillacs. Supreme Motorcars."

"Yeah," he said. "That's right. That's where it was."

The two other policemen walked up and I noticed how their

uniforms were different, that they were from outside Nashville. Franklin, I decided. Why were two cops from another county here in Nashville? Wasn't this supposedly outside their jurisdiction?

A tow truck pulled up followed by a man in a Porsche, one of those babies that cost about as much as every house in the entire neighborhood we were standing in put together, and he walked over to the circle of officers and everybody engaged in a conversation. They were so occupied I almost thought I could stroll off and go back home to my bed, but then I thought how they might see me fleeing the scene of the crime and be compelled to shoot me in the back like Gloria Swanson blew away William Holden in Sunset Boulevard. Anyway, in my own stupid way, I didn't want to take off and leave Jennifer all alone. I'm a gallant one, all right.

In a minute the group headed toward Jennifer and me, which I thought was the preamble to her having to walk a straight line and blow into a bottle and me getting the crap beaten out of me just for general principle. Instead, the two men in the car were polite and respectful and told Jennifer how they were glad she wasn't hurt and how her car would get pulled from the ditch and there'd be no problem with any of the property damages tonight, for it had already all been taken care of. The four policemen stood by watching the wrecker hook up with the car and waited until it got pulled out, then they all headed for their patrol cars and sat inside them for a while filling out reports, while Jennifer talked to the man in the Porsche and nodded her head at everything he said and I stood by wondering if my services were still required. That was when she told the man in the Porsche that she didn't need a ride home, thank you, but my friend will take me home, hooking her arm through mine like we were just made to be together this magical evening.

Needless to say, by this time I was thoroughly confused and fairly bewildered by what I'd been watching transpire since I'd rushed down here from my cozy bed. First of all I'd been told this accident happened mainly because Jennifer was driving by my house to see if I was home or out with some other woman, which sounded like borderline jealousy to me, which seemed highly improbable that a girl like her would be wasting time wondering about a loser like me, and then there was her Mercedes in a ditch with police arriving to crawl all over the scene, followed by the two out of county cops who'd come by to curtail the investigation until the stranger in the Carrera drove up and set everybody straight and assigned what had to be done to solve this problem to the officers who were more than glad not to ask any more questions or perform any sobriety tests or place anybody under arrest or even beat the hell out of me for having the audacity to be present in the first place, and in the final part of the encounter there was the head honcho of the night's festivities driving away in his gold Porsche and there was Jennifer left with me to walk back up the street and get my Civic to drive her home.

Yeah, it made a whole lot of sense to me.

"I'm glad Teresa was able to get in touch with John so fast," Jennifer said when we were in the Civic and pulling out of the driveway. "That didn't turn out anywhere near as bad as I thought it might."

I didn't say anything much, but I was starting to understand by then. Jennifer had called her aunt and Teresa had called John and John had pulled some strings with his amigos down at City Hall, and two of the county's finest had hightailed it down 65 North to the scene of the wreck to provide some advance protection until the militia in the Porsche arrived on the scene. From what I'd seen, whoever the dude in the expensive German automobile had been he was at the least pretty important and at the most might have been Ernst Stavro Blofield and was the head of some department who would destroy what was in its path first and answer no questions about it later. I'm not the most savvy guy around, but it didn't take a whole lot of schooling to see that money and power had just got through talking and laying out the rules, and that was why Jennifer Payne was on her way home with me as if nothing much had happened, as if all of this that had gone down after the Fourth of July fireworks had exploded and everyone had gone to bed was all in a night's work.

When we got to Jennifer's condo my uncle and Teresa were waiting for us out in the lot. Not only was I surprised to see my uncle and step-aunt together, but I was also amazed at how professional the two of them seemed, like they were accustomed to going through rough stretches together and were unfazed by it all. It was strange as hell to me. It was like everything I had learned about the two of them and how maybe my uncle wasn't the salt of the earth as I'd assumed for so long and how Teresa maybe wasn't this woman with the romantic past that had just caught up with Sam Thornton and brought back the magic she'd had to abandon for so long didn't matter as much as I thought it should, and how maybe it was I still didn't comprehend the levels of life wherein people dwell with their money and their power and their status that folks like me who have never ventured there for too long a spell don't know any of the rules or how they got applied from one moment to another.

"Are you all right?" Teresa asked. "You're not hurt from the accident in any way, are you?"

"I'm fine," Jennifer said. "Just tired and a little stressed, that's all. I'd really like to go to bed."

"You don't have to worry about anything," Uncle John said. "It's all been taken care of." He looked at me like he couldn't understand what I was doing there. I don't think he had any inkling about Jennifer and me up until then.

"Leonard," he said. "Fancy meeting you here."

"Jennifer and Leonard are friends," Teresa explained. "I introduced them at the Thanksgiving party. One thing begat another, I suppose, so here they are."

"Well," John smiled, "I guess if your mother calls me wondering what you've been up to lately, I'll just tell her I haven't the slightest idea."

"Leonard lives just down the street from where I had my accident," Jennifer yawned. "He was nice enough to come down and hang out with me so I wouldn't have to be alone."

"It was three in the morning," I said. "It wasn't like I had anything better to do."

On the way home the sun was beginning to rise. I was trying to decide whether to go home or stop at a Waffle House and have breakfast and coffee like I had a busy day ahead of me and needed the carbs, but what I did was drive by Sam's place to see if his car was there, and when I spotted the Tiger parked in the drive, I felt a little better. At least he wasn't alone this night. He'd had at least one of his true loves nearby, the one with a four-speed who'd been with him all along.

· · · ·

In the dreamworld I'd grown up in, Jennifer Payne would have called me up the next morning and pledged her love to me forever for saving her skin the previous evening, but that didn't happen. As a matter of fact, I didn't hear from Jennifer again for a couple of weeks, and the only reason I talked to her then was because I was the one who called her to see if she was dead or not. You would have thought, after engaging in conversation with her for a few minutes, that the night in question with the car in the ditch and the police and the mysterious man in the Porsche had never happened. It was like I was the only one who had any inkling about it, and maybe it was I'd only dreamed the whole thing and it had never happened.

Sam explained it to me on our lunch break later on. This is what a woman does, he assured me, especially women who are accustomed to being sheltered by money.

"I don't know too much about her family other than what Teresa has said about growing up," Sam said, "how her own parents and Jennifer's mother died and there was a lot of insurance money and money for child support from Jennifer's father after he and her mother divorced, so I don't think Jennifer or Teresa as her guardian along with her marriage to John Wright had to ever want for anything. I'm not saying they were all that wealthy, but they for damn sure weren't living in abject poverty. I'm pretty sure nobody ever had to save money for clothes or a new car or anything. At least not like you and me, partner. I don't think either Teresa or Jennifer ever had any inkling of what it's like to be really broke."

I still hadn't told Sam about Teresa's hand in Jennifer walking away free after the wreck. I know very well what kept me from saying anything—Sam was always so sold on Teresa's devotion to him, this notion of undying love he was certain the two of them possessed for each other—that he couldn't imagine her being in any kind of cooperative dealings with her husband. He hadn't come right out and said it aloud, but there was something in the way he stayed patient and waited for Teresa to finish up whatever embroil-Ralph ment she was in as the wife of John Wright and move on to free herself of bearing his name that made me believe Sam would wait forever for her to do so, and so I didn't want to upset him by rocking the boat and saying it was possible that all he was waiting for and believing in might never happen. Anyway, I was younger than him and hadn't been around the way he had, so what did I know? I thought it was better to keep my trap shut and let wiser folks than me go on with their travels down Life's highways without me telling them the wrong exit to take. I decided to forgive Jennifer for not giving me any credit in her survival against the forces of the law and simply try and reassert myself into her life again. After all, I asked myself, where was I going to find a woman with her looks in my corner of the world? I would do better, I decided, to roll with the punches and ignore her ingratitude and the fact that she had taken full advantage of her ties to wealth to get away with a deed that would have landed any other average person in the slammer, behavior I ordinarily would not tolerate much. I tried not to con-sider what would have happened had I landed my Civic in a ditch along with someone's mailbox after downing beer beforehand, and how if that had been the case I would probably be in some form of Folsom Prison this very moment getting all excited because Johnny Cash was coming for a concert. I didn't really have to like Jennifer Payne so much, I mused; all I really had to do was position myself to be around her physical presence so I could get my hands on her and secure some kind of sexual contact I'd only dreamed of when I was younger and let all the other facets ride. It was like I was complain-ing because I was getting too much cake for dessert. I told myself how if I had known this opportunity would be coming my way when I became an adult I wouldn't have wasted so much time being a kid.

I also knew I wasn't the only guy pursuing Jennifer these days. There were other richer and more elegant men on her scent, and I knew I probably wouldn't be the one coming out the winner in the end, but that wasn't so important to me right then. What was important was that sometimes, unlike most of my previous life, I wasn't alone on an evening. I had a choice in the matter. Some-times I actually had a real live girl who was on television and was there at my side for everyone to notice, and because of that maybe the world might decide that I wasn't so much of a failure after all. It didn't matter whether I liked this girl much or not. What mattered was I might be seen as someone who was maybe not so pathetic as first thought. Maybe the world would think there was more to me than what I'd shown so far.

No, it certainly wasn't a flaming romance between Jennifer and me, but it was at least for a time convenient to us both. I think having a normal fellow like me around was comforting to Jennifer, much more so than the upper class set with their high-tier jobs and their money and expensive clothes she'd seen so much of before me. The truth was she didn't have to try so hard with me. There wasn't so much she had to live up to. It was as if knowing she was the prettiest girl I'd ever dated or been around my entire life made her feel special in a sense, something a little more than just beautiful and an object of sexual desire. I was somebody she could let her guard down to and actually be herself for a change.

She even skirted the issue once, although I'm sure she didn't really mean to give her innermost feelings such a public airing.

"The good thing about you," she told me on our way back from a Cher concert one night, "is I don't ever have to think twice about anything when you're around. I don't have to act like I'm a big star who's on television or anything like that. I can just throw on some comfortable clothes and go out and eat a cheeseburger and that's fine with you. I don't have to get all dressed up and mind my manners and eat something expensive I don't really like." I wasn't really sure how to answer that. I didn't know whether I should feel flattered or insulted.

"Well," I countered, "at least you don't start throwing up when I come around. I suppose I can take solace in that."

"Oh, no, I like you," she smiled. "In fact, that's what I really like about you. I don't have to worry about money and pretense and stuff with you. That's what I keep telling Aunt Teresa about her problems with John and Sam. She likes Sam more than John, but John has money and is the pathway to what she wants in the world, while Sam is a dead end when it comes to stuff like that. I keep telling her that someday she's going to have to make a choice between Sam and John. She's going to have to choose between being happy or safe. She can't stay in-between the two of them forever."

"I don't know that she'll ever be as safe as she wants with Sam Thornton," I said.

"I think she knows that," Jennifer said. "I think right now she's in the middle of trying to figure out exactly what she wants from the world when it all comes down to it, and how to be happy when she finally gets it."

Seven

The Dog Days arrived and the afternoons and nights grew heavy with heat and humidity. Most days after closing time my uniform shirt would be soaked with sweat, even after staying in my air-conditioned work area all day, for there would inevitably come a time when a car would have to be taken outside for a test drive, and that would be all it would take for scorching temperatures to find their way under my shirt and take residence on the pores of my skin. Maybe Nashville had always been this way while I was growing up, but I couldn't help thinking that the atmosphere was filled these days with a deadly form of heat I'd never encountered until this particular summer.

From all I could tell, Sam and Teresa were heating up more each day as well. I was informed on one of my infrequent dates with Jennifer that this entire summer Teresa had not gone on any of her usual excursions or taken any cruises, but had elected instead to stay in town because of the intensity of her relationship with Sam. I'm almost afraid for her, Jennifer confided, because she doesn't seem to have any caution to her behavior these days. It's as if she either doesn't care to hide it anymore or she just isn't able to keep it under wraps. I'm afraid if she's not careful something bad is going to come out of all of this.

On the other hand, I couldn't tell what Sam was thinking. Because we were so busy at work, lots of times there was no opportunity to take an hour for lunch and engage in any kind of conversation between ourselves. The work crew mostly ate sandwiches brought in from nearby restaurants so no one would waste time eating and fall behind the promised times for cars to be ready for pickup. Most days I was covered up with work, given assignments to work on cars that I hadn't been allowed to touch several months before, and because I was so busy concentrating on doing a good job and not screwing anything up, each day went by so fast I could hardly believe it. I think it was that way with every mechanic working at Wright's.

Sam was no exception, though he could handle the onslaught of work better than the rest of us. He never had to take time to look things up on the computer, consult manuals, or watch a YouTube video on how to perform a procedure, because he already knew all that information by heart. It was second nature to him. He could have authored all the manuals himself if he'd been so inclined, and the consensus from the customers soon rose to a tide of the majority preferring Sam to exclusively work on their vehicles, and they would get on a waiting list for that to happen rather than allow one of us lesser talents to fix their problem. It was during this hubbub of summertime activity that my uncle first found out about Sam and Teresa. Maybe he'd had an idea something was going on with his wife for some time by then, but I think it surprised him that it involved one of his own employees. I'm not certain when any of this came about, but Jennifer said that Teresa told her it had happened. At first Jennifer had been frightened at what consequences might ensue because of this discovery, but Teresa had taken it with a dash of salt, saying she wasn't too concerned what her husband knew or thought, that what went on between them had been going on long before this. Listening to this discourse, the whole scene reminded me of one of the movies I watched on Turner Classics, and the more I thought about it the more my Step-Aunt Teresa began to resemble a bad and guilty Lana Turner in The Postman Always Rings Twice, and sure enough, several times after going to bed late at night my personal Lana would visit me in my drowsy state and tell me how she'd been misunderstood all those times after being branded as bad. Everything I did I did for love, she would state, so I don't see why I should be blamed for what I had in my heart. Tell me Leonard, if it were you and me, wouldn't you have done the same?

The bottom line was my uncle had discovered Teresa was having an affair, but the question was did he actually know who she was carrying on with? I knew if he found out for certain it was Sam, then, great mechanic or not, Sam would be fired immediately and the elite would just have to get used to the fact that their cars would have to get worked on by someone else. With this newfound knowledge I made it a point to let Sam know what might be coming his way, just so he could make plans to break everything off or get more discreet or even leave town if he thought hired killers would be coming soon to see him. This thought, again, came to me during my moments of fanciful thinking, as if life here in Nashville and its adjoining communities was a microcosm of what I'd grown up seeing in film noir movies. In my head, if one indulged in illicit behavior with a woman who belonged to a ruthless higher-statured person, it was almost a given that Barton MacLane or Lee Marvin or some other tough was going to make an appearance at their door and offer some licks from brass knuckles or brandish a gun and wound or kill the indulger and some sort of criminal justice would thus be served. In my more lucid moments I told myself happenings like this didn't really take place in the civilized real world, but all it would take was to turn on the nightly news or pick up a paper and read about some gruesome local murder and I'd be right back into my black foreboding mode again.

I couldn't keep quiet about it anymore. On a Sunday afternoon I drove to Sam's and told him what I'd learned. I couldn't stand the idea of him coming in to work the next morning and having a couple of goons waiting there for him to read him his rights and set him straight.

I wasn't expecting the reaction I got. Sam looked at me like I was from another planet and didn't understand the way things worked here on earth. I felt like he was having to become some sort of kindergarten teacher who had to explain to an innocent child the way the world functioned most days of the week.

"John Wright would have to be either blind or dead not to know what was going on with Teresa," he told me. "How could he not notice his wife being gone most of the time without adding two and two together? Heck, just the fact that they're not sleeping together ought to be enough to at least pique his curiosity, since here he is married to a woman twenty-five years younger than him, and he'd have to know a woman that age wasn't going to live a life of chaste denial for too long. All he'd have to do is look in the mirror and consider what he'd been up to himself to know something might be going on."

"You have to know he was going to find out sooner or later."

"The thing, Leonard, is this." Sam leaned forward in his

chair and folded his hands. It was as if he was expressing one of the major truths in the world and me and everyone else should get down to the business of accepting it, because it is what it is and all the discussion in the world was never going to change it. "Sooner or later your damn uncle is going to have to know the truth. He's going to have to come to grips with the fact that his marriage is over and Teresa and I are going to end up together. I mean, I know there are going to be some hard feelings and some real fireworks and rocky times, and in the end I know I won't be employed at his business anymore, but that's just the way it is, Leonard. That's to be expected. It's not like something of this sort hasn't happened before in the history of the planet. Couples break up all the time and everybody goes their separate ways. That's the way it is out in the real world."

"Maybe it is, but if you ask me it still seems like a good way to get a bullet in your gut."

"Once again, you're worrying too much. It gets in the way of rational thought."

"I just never have been a fan of messing with anything that could up and get me killed."

"You don't understand. When you come to realize there's a plan for everything, well, that's when everything starts coming into focus." Sam grinned at me like I was lost in the woods and it was his job to bring me back into the fold. "You want a cup of coffee or anything? Why don't you settle back in your chair and I'll tell you a little story, and maybe when I finish everything will become crystal clear to you. You'll be all up to date with what's going on in this mean old world we live in."

He heated some water and mixed me a cup of Folger's Instant, and I nestled in to listen to the story of the world as Sam Thornton saw it.

"I told you about my dad dying when I was thirteen. He didn't leave us in much of a good place when he passed, me and my two sisters and my mother, who was pretty damn sick herself but still trying to work. There was no pension coming in from my dad's days as a mechanic, and he hadn't lived long enough to qualify for Social Security. The way it ended up was my sister of seventeen had to go to work full-time at Kroger trying to bring in money and save up enough to go to college, and my other sister who was fifteen couldn't do anything but babysit, and then there was me, thirteen, full of piss and oats, wanting to play football and basketball and someday become a Hollywood star on top of that, and all I could do was cut yards, and the only thing I had left as an inheritance from my father was his 1965 Sunbeam Tiger project car that hadn't seen the highway in years because he never had enough money at one time to get it roadworthy. But he'd loved that Tiger, I knew that. I used to hang around the garage and watch him work on it, hoping that one day it would be a hundred percent restored and that some distant time in the future it would be mine, but he'd died before that day came. What happened was the Tiger was the only thing left from him that I got to keep for myself, and so for all the years to come I did exactly that. I took it with me wherever I went, thinking the day was going to arrive when I would get it to the level my dad had always wanted it to get to. But shit happened, Leonard, to me the same way it had to him, like it does to everybody, I suspect. I tried working my way through school using the money I made from peddling pot, but I got caught finally, and when that happened I lost everything I'd ever managed to accumulate. I lost all the money I had paying fines and lawyers, and then I lost a block of my life getting locked up. I became a felon, and let me tell you, I found out the world doesn't look too kindly on a fellow with a record. They don't want him as their neighbor or to hire him for a job or have him go to school to get a degree along with all the other decent people of society. Especially they don't want him coming anywhere near their daughter, and all those daughters don't really want him around either, because they know a guy with a record is mean and dirty and only after one thing in the end, the one thing in the world he understands, the ugly and vile portion, so it's best to stay away from him and give him a wide passage, to keep away from his hands and his eyes so nothing bad will come of it. That's the way it was with me. That's what I learned, Leonard. The world wrote me off and stuck a label on me I couldn't erase. Do not touch. Keep your distance. Both my sisters were that way toward me when I got out, and I wonder if my mother would have been the same way if she'd still been alive. When I looked for Teresa after I got out of jail, she'd already left school and was gone back home somewhere—Atlanta, I think, I was never sure—and I figured she'd gotten married or gone off to be in the movies or something, some place where her good looks would open doors for her, and I never knew how or where to look for her after that. It was like she'd vanished off the face of the earth, or at least that part of the earth I knew. It wasn't the way it is now. You couldn't just type her name in a computer and have it instantly tell you where she was.

"Though that didn't stop me from looking for her everywhere I went for a while, even if I never did admit to myself that was what I was doing. I moved around from city to city, big and small towns, working whatever jobs I could come across at private garages and big franchises, renting rooms and apartments and never sticking around long enough to really settle in, until it got to be not so much about making money or finding Teresa or discovering a place where I felt like I belonged. It was normal to be throwing my bags in the Sunbeam's trunk and heading down the interstate to somewhere else. Most times I didn't even have a destination in mind when I was leaving. It was just natural to be on the move, going until my money ran low and it was time to stop and start somewhere new again. Heck, it even got to where I felt funny if I hung around a place too long. I'd start getting the heebie jeebies and take off for no reason whatsoever, just because that was the state of normal I'd come to know and feel comfortable within. After so much time passed it wasn't like I was looking for Teresa or any kind of peaceful life anymore; Teresa was just something from way back when that had happened and had held centerstage for a while until time finally swept it away and replaced it with something else. You know how it is, Leonard. You can probably come up with a million things in your lifetime you once thought were so important, and now they don't mean jack shit. That's the way life is, buddy. The older you get the truer it is. Everything's like telephone poles on the highway, appearing and coming at you and then going by until you can't keep up with them anymore and it's like they never existed. They all look alike and they all disappear in a hurry, and after a while there's nothing about them you remember.

"That's why it got to me so much when I saw Teresa again after so long. It was like I'd forgotten about her and the past and that one night we had together, and time had done its thing and taken me into undiscovered countries and unknown highways, and I was doing what I'd always done for so many years since I was a kid, walking around at another in an endless procession of car shows, looking at other people's finished projects all shiny bright with new engines and transmissions and showroom tires without a mile of tread on them and spanking new interiors to sit in and custom steering wheels that you could drive away to most anywhere in if you pleased, and I was eyeing another heavenly two-seater when I looked up and Teresa was there after a thousand years of being absent, there in front of me like she'd been around all the time. I watched her for I don't know how long. I couldn't decide if the woman before me was who I thought she was, or if she was simply someone who looked like somebody I used to know. I watched her for a long time trying to decide if I was hallucinating. When I finally determined seeing was believing I knew I'd have to somehow find out why she was here at a classic sports car show and what she was doing, what kind of life she'd been leading since that one night we shared, and if because I'd finally run across her again did it mean it was in the stars that the two of us were to be together and our time had come around again. All sorts of nutty ideas went through my head, I don't have the fingers to count them with. I had wild notions about how my life was going to change and how everything was going to be different now that I'd found Teresa Payne again. I had it all worked out in my head within ten minutes, about the time it took to finish following her and the old guy she was with around the yard, to know that all the information I needed was to have her address and to learn what name she was going by these days and then fate would take care of the rest. The only concoction that needed to be added to the mix was for me to be dropped in, and then the components would join and come together and everything would be as it had originally been intended.

"So," he smiled, "I figured once I accumulated all the necessary facts, I could then put my scheme in motion. I walked behind her and the man, stopping and looking at every car on display in great detail, following her from section to section and even into an area where there were food booths and tables and chairs where the two of them sat down and had lunch. I sat at another table fifteen feet away and ate a cheeseburger. I wondered if Teresa was going to look my way and recognize me after all the years, and one time she did look right at me and I thought for certain she knew it was me, but I guess nothing clicked in her memory right then. I supposed she was probably a lot like me, going to some unconnected place where she never expected Sam Thornton to pop up or to see me all of a sudden out of the blue when for so long the idea was lodged in her mind that she'd gone this long and she'd never see me again."

By the time he'd gotten this far with his story and his history of Teresa and him and their lost romance I was beginning to wonder if everything he'd told me was true in the real sense or if the major- ity of it had only gone on in his imagination. I could understand if that's the way it was, for it would be exactly like something I might do myself under like circumstances.

"Anyway," he summed up, "what I'm saying is there's sim- ply way too much coincidence in all this for me to believe that my running across Teresa again is just an accident. If there's such a thing as a Providence up in the sky directing the stars and causing all the pieces to fall in place, then count me in as a firm believer, because that's exactly the way this is. And it's also my belief that a man has to be a pure fool not to see the answers to the big puzzle when they're served right on the plate before him. A fellow would have to be blind not to notice." "Yeah, I said, "maybe that's so, but you've got to be careful too. I'm just trying to keep you from getting plugged by a shotgun shell, that's all. Heck, for all we know something like that may be written in the stars too."

I could see I couldn't change his mind. Even though he was older and supposedly wiser than me, and I was just this young coun- terpart who'd barely escaped kid status by now, it wasn't hard to recognize that I was the only one of us who was having rational thoughts. It was going to take something more than my harping, some kind of intelligent wave of reason from some higher source to change Sam Thornton's viewpoint about him and Teresa Payne- Wright and the way the planet spun on course and caused everything to transpire the way it had once from the beginning been deemed to do.

I thought about my own dealings with Jennifer over the past months, and how like Sam I too might start believing something special had been ordained for me and her, but I knew better. I wasn't that far gone. I was just this guy who'd lucked upon a pretty girl by blind chance, and once I'd been around her for a while it had come to me that perhaps she wasn't as pretty as I'd first thought, that maybe she was a lot like me, and in the end neither of us were all that much to brag about.

. . . .

I knew something was in the works on the morning Scotty Rawls stopped me by the coffee machine and wanted to know how often Sam and I went out for beers after work and how well I really knew him. I didn't really know how to answer this or if I even ought to try, but it all came about so fast that all I did was shrug my shoulders and reply, "Now and then," and let it go at that. I didn't think right that moment to ask why Scotty was so interested in what Sam and I did after work hours, but I found out soon enough what this was all about.

Scotty's wife worked parttime at the shop on Saturdays, manning the front counter so Doris could have the weekend off. The shop closed at noon on Saturdays, so most of the mechanics took that day off, but there was always a skeleton crew around to take care of whatever emergency problems might arise. I hardly recall Sam ever being around for one of these half days, and if he was, it wasn't on any kind of a regular basis. That's why it seemed strange to me when I caught wind of the rumor that Sam and Scotty's wife Melinda had some kind of affair going, since I had never seen the two of them together at the same time for all the months I'd been around. I heard two mechanics say something about it and didn't really connect what they were talking about, and then the day came when Scotty walked into Sam's workspace and the two of them had words. I wasn't around to take any of it in, but Sam had denied any of it and wondered of Scotty where he might have gotten such an idea. Scotty merely told him how he wasn't a fool and that Sam better watch his step from there on.

"You need to tell John what's going on," I suggested.

Sam and I were sitting on the patio at a Logan's, drinking beer and eating shelled peanuts from a miniature metal bin that looked like a trash can. It was the day after Scotty had confronted Sam at work, and in the twenty-four hours since it occurred there had been a deadly calm come over the garage that made the canned music from the ceiling speakers sound like the performers were there on the premises and had the amps and the mikes turned up full decibel so no one in the audience would miss a lick. Usually, the sound of work being done, the whirr of drills, the clatter of tools dropped on the concrete floor, phones ringing and procedures being explained, overrode the music and let an observer know he was within a place of professional workmanship. For that one day the silence was so overwhelming it was impossible not to believe a storm was on its way.

"I don't know what in the hell I need to tell him," Sam said. "Scotty Rawls has been with him for a long time, and if your uncle doesn't know he's crazy by now it's not up to me to educate him. The fact that I don't even know the guy's wife ought to account for something, but I guess it's true you just can't beat hearsay and gossip when it comes down to cases. If the dude says I've been porking his wife, then I guess I'm supposed to own up to it and promise not to ever do it again. Hell, I just told him he had a bee up his ass and couldn't tell the difference in what was real or what was bullshit. That's when he threatened me and told me how he was going to get me in the end."

I knew Sam was telling the truth about Scotty's wife and not knowing her, because I couldn't hardly come up with a Saturday that Sam and her had been at the shop together, and if they hadn't crossed paths in that venue the odds were they'd never even seen each other anywhere before. Somehow Scotty had been given misinformation by someone who'd decided to create this story for some strange type of entertainment, but I didn't know where to start to look for the culprit. I ended up deciding to mind my own business and let it go, thinking something so unwarranted would surely fade away in time and all would go on as it had before.

. . . .

Of course, I was wrong. On Sunday night, while I was watching My Darling Clementine and getting myself psyched to go back to work in the morning, my phone started buzzing. I looked and saw it was Sam calling and almost let him leave a message so I wouldn't have to miss the big showdown with Wyatt Earp and the Clantons or deal with any of the other drama the world was putting forth lately, but because Sam never called me much at all these days I was curious as to why he was ringing me now, so I pressed the answer icon and said hello.

"I've got some weird shit going on," he said.

"What weird shit?"

"A couple of guys in a pickup truck started following me tonight when I was going to meet Teresa. I could tell they were after me because they weren't the least bit covert about their actions. They just got right up on my butt and started flashing their lights and sounding the horn for a couple of blocks and motioning for me to pull over. Well, I knew better than that, so I started taking a bunch of side streets and turning down corners and made my way to the interstate and ran the speedometer up to about 110 and headed out of town. When I couldn't see them anymore I pulled off and called Teresa to let her know I wasn't coming and then started making my way back to town using the back streets, going about ten miles out of my way just to avoid my new friends. I wasn't about to go home because I figured they'd be there waiting for me. I'm not exactly sure what's going on, Leonard, but I'd bet our friend Scotty is at the bottom of this. I wasn't really close enough to tell, but I'd lay down the deed to the ranch it was him in the passenger seat of the truck that was trying to run me down."

"I wonder who put the idea that you were running around with his wife in his head? It doesn't make sense to me."

"I've got a theory about that. I'm thinking that whoever told him such a thing is doing it for another reason entirely. Tell me, if you were a rich and powerful big shot and some joker was fooling around with your wife, would you take the chance on confronting him yourself? I don't think so. You'd let somebody else take care of it for you. What I think is once somebody found out about me and Teresa they went straight to John Wright and spilled the beans, and whether or not he and Teresa have an open marriage or not or don't give the first diddlyshit about each other doesn't matter in this case. What matters is appearances, and your kindly old Uncle John simply can't have his upstanding loyal wife hooked up with a nobody from nowhere that no one knows anything about other than that the guy knows how to fix broken-down sports cars, because if something like that was to get out then it wouldn't look good to all the boards John's on or to any of the clubs he's in or might come between some of the business and political relationships he's nurtured over the years. Guys like this don't like being the objects of gossip, and they for damn sure aren't happy when their dirty laundry gets aired and hung out on the clothesline for public viewing."

"You think John is behind this?"

"I don't think, buddy, I know."

"Where does Scotty Rawls come in on all this?"

"Somebody's convinced him I'm screwing his wife on the side. I don't know if she's actually having an affair with somebody and I'm a mistaken identity, but I seriously doubt that. I think somebody's told Scotty that I'm the guilty party so he'll take care of me one way or another, and I think it's this way so somebody— namely, your Uncle John—won't get his hands dirty getting rid of me himself. That's the way these dudes operate, Leonard. They just move figures around on their chess board and let the pieces fall in place without ever getting mixed up in the fray. I've seen this shit go on too many times before not to recognize it now."

I'd seen it too, only not in real life, but mainly on Turner Classics when they were featuring a noir film and some John Garfield-type gets played for a fool by a rich crime boss who's got a girlfriend that looks like Veronica Lake. I'd watched such scenes a hundred times, and I knew that most of the time the poor sap gets beaten up or plugged by a .45 or played for a fool by the doll with blonde hair and big blue eyes, eyes you positively knew were blue even though the movie was in black and white. I could sense the same thing in my head right now, just as sure as if I was home in my bedroom watching it on my 32-inch TV. I could see Uncle John making a phone call, hanging up and smiling at the thought of the wheels he'd just set in motion, and then lighting up a cigarette to go along with the cocktail he held in his hands. It was life imitating art, or maybe the other way around, but in the end I didn't know how I could help out the John Garfield on the screen or my friend Sam on the other end of the cellphone call.

．．．．

The more I thought about it the more I knew Sam was right. I'd already been provided too many clues that my uncle wasn't the best man on the face of the earth, what with his cloudy marriage to Teresa and the shady political company he kept and his rumored dark associations with some of the crookedest organizations in the state. It wasn't difficult to determine that he was a guy who wasn't exactly stellar in the sense of how my generation had been taught to be growing up, but more the fact that he was one of those bad people who'd sold out in the beginning and took a place in the world holding the reins on people who were working hard and trying to do the right thing. I didn't know it for a fact, because my dad never discussed family skeletons with me, but I'd heard the rumors down through the years of how my uncle had pocketed the family wealth for himself when my grandparents died, that he had been the executor of the estate and made certain most of the tangible portions went to him, and that was how he'd mounted his bankroll in the first place. My dad and my aunts were led to trust their older brother and be content with what he'd deemed to give them. I wondered if he had told everyone he was investing the lion's share of the estate into stocks and bonds and businesses wherein the entire family would always be taken care of in the future, but so far I had seen no sign of that. Anyway, John had been the big brother they all idolized and looked up to, and they'd believed what he'd told them, but I had come to the opinion that even if we were kin and I was held in his employ there were still not many things or beliefs the two of us held in common. I didn't want to appear ungrateful after what my uncle had done for me these past months, giving me a job and providing me with a pathway where I might hobnob with a class of people I would in my old life never have had the chance to rub elbows with, but that didn't explain everything. I thought of Jennifer and how if I hadn't been present at an employee holiday celebration I never would have met her, much less had the chance to get my working class/rehabilitation paws on her. It all came about because of me being John Wright's nephew, but sometimes things and events become too large to ignore. You can't trust a person all the way down the line.

What I didn't know was the extent of what had happened that early evening that Sam hadn't gone into detail about. Yes, he had mentioned the two men in the truck and the aggressive manner they had followed him and attempted to have him pull over, and he had mentioned how one of the men in the truck appeared to be Scotty Rawls and that he suspected Scotty had been primed to do him some physical harm because he'd been fed lies about his wife and Sam by someone who had an ulterior motive, so it wasn't so hard for me to connect the dots on all that, but the absolute totality of what had happened during the ensuing race between the two men in the truck and Sam in his Sunbeam Tiger had not been explained fully by Sam, who perhaps didn't want to worry me too much or was in such a precarious plight at the moment of his call that he hadn't time to tell me any more sordid details before he thought it wise to move on again.

The men in the truck had first cornered him at a traffic light at an intersection close to downtown, and Sam had cut the Tiger's wheel to make a hard left and go back the opposite way, a U-turn in traffic that had people honking their horns and wondering what kind of madman was behind the wheel of the funny-looking sports car tearing down Church Street like it was running from a bolt of lightning. When the pickup truck turned left and performed the same maneuver the car had done, the people at the lights knew something was up, and some picked up their phones and dialed the police to report an ongoing incident. It was not every Sunday evening, even in crime-ridden downtown Nashville, that wild occurrences such as they'd just witnessed went on before their very eyes. This kind of stuff was reserved for movies or television or video games, not right there in the open where innocent people might get hurt.

The chase had gone on for almost ten minutes, down back

streets and across parking lots and even speeding at one time down a dead-end street, scattering people walking from their condos to dinner or out on the sidewalks allowing their dogs to stretch their legs and take a peaceful tinkle. Even on a slow news time on a Sunday evening tweets and emails were sent to the TV stations with reports of wild violence happening on the city streets, and sirens sounded and reporters were dispatched to cover what might turn out to be a big story in the making.

Like Chuck Berry's V-8 Ford, nothing was up to catching Sam and Ophelia once they found an open road, and when Sam came to a ramp for I-65 he swerved onto it and passed a slow-moving panel truck to enter. Horns blared and birds were shot as he passed the outgoing highway traffic as if they were parked there in their inside lanes, and for ten minutes he kept the speedometer above one hundred as he passed exit after exit, sailing through Brentwood and Franklin and on past Spring Hill until the sun had finished setting and there were only headlights far behind him in the night. That was when he'd pulled off into a Cracker Barrel parking lot and given me a call, and it wasn't until later that I realized he'd only phoned to give me a head's up that trouble might be knocking at my door any minute. He hadn't wanted me to get unknowingly involved in any of this brouhaha he'd found himself mysteriously embroiled in.

He'd not gone home that Sunday night for a while, opting to sit and eat a fried chicken dinner at the Cracker Barrel and drink numerous cups of coffee while deciding what to do next. It wasn't in him to get spooked over such a turn of events, but he felt like the best thing to do now was to lay low for a little until he decided who exactly the enemy was and why they would want physical harm directed his way. Every way he looked at it, the answer always came out to be good old John Wright, pillar of the community, good Christian businessman, and a friend to all.

A little before midnight he drove back to Nashville and circled the block around his duplex, looking for the truck or a strange car that might be waiting for him. All seemed quiet, so he parked and went inside and tried to grab a few hours' sleep until morning.

• • • •

I didn't exactly know what to expect when I arrived at work on Monday morning. By the time I got there I hadn't heard anything more about the action that had gone on Sunday night, but I did suspect there was bound to be some kind of residue from Scotty's prior threats and the appearance of the hostile truck that had followed Sam when he'd first left home. I guess what I was expecting was for Scotty to still be in a blind rage wanting to attack Sam physically the first instant he came upon him, but that's not the way it happened at all. What went down was everything was eerily quiet all the way up to lunchtime. The shop emptied out like it always did for an hour with most of the crew crossing the street to eat at the Boulevard Grille, which was a meat and three that made a killing off the businesses that lined that section of town, while some of the more economically-minded stayed behind and ate their lunch in the breakroom and enjoyed a little peace and quiet reading the newspaper or one of the magazines that were scattered about.

I wandered as I generally did down to the doors that said Employees Only and cracked it open to see if Sam was there. I hate to admit what a chicken and a disloyal friend I was, but the truth is I was halfway afraid Scotty might be inside waiting for Sam or else might just appear any minute, and I didn't necessarily want to be in the middle of what might go on. It wasn't so much like I was Simon Peter reincarnated and felt the need to deny any association with Sam in order to save my own sorry skin, but it was a direct result of the lessons I'd personally learned down through the years, those times where I'd found myself screwed-up profusely for taking the wrong side in a dispute or believing what someone told me was the gospel and then finding out later it was just another line of bull and I'd have to pay the price for being fool enough to believe it. Sam had indeed become my friend and confidant and mentor all in one for almost half a year now, but there was still a part of me that was hesitant to yield myself over to his personality one hundred percent. I wasn't so certain the Sam Thornton I knew was the real authentic personage, or if he was only some variety of parts I had assembled little by little in my head to fulfill my needs and help me along in a world I'd thus far never before been able to keep secure footing in, fixed it so Sam Thornton would become the classic main character

I generally saw on Turner Classics and I could become his trusted sidekick, the one who is around for the duration of the show but is never the person the all-too serious plot revolves around.

Sam was there all right. He was sitting at a table by himself with a cup of vending machine coffee, not eating at all, but simply sitting and studying the cardboard cup the machine had dropped down for him like there was some secret writing etched upon it that contained the answers to everything a fellow would ever want to know. He looked up and saw me and grinned, then went back to studying his cup again.

"Come on in," he said. "I'm glad to see a friendly face. I was expecting any minute Scotty and his henchman to come bursting in with guns a'blazin'."

"I come in peace, Kemosabe."

"After the last twenty-four hours I'm beginning to think such a concept as peace doesn't exist anymore." He picked up his coffee and drained the last of it, made a face over just how bad a cup of coffee could possibly get. "I'm starting to become accustomed to threats of violence and wild car chases."

He told me about the previous evening, and I wondered how he'd even been able to sleep after an ordeal like that or how he had talked himself into showing up this morning after such an experience. Had it been me, I would still be driving away from Nashville and its environs, heading for a safe faraway place in Phoenix or Albuquerque or Oklahoma that Glen Campbell used to sing about, someplace totally removed and distant where the life that had gone south wasn't around anymore.

I knew there was something he wanted to say, but there were others sitting around who looked like they were equipped with ears for listening, so he motioned to me and we went out the door and down the hallway to the side of the building. There was a picnic table set up outside, and we sat down under the shade of the trees.

"A funny thing happened last night I wasn't the least bit used to," he said. "In the process of making myself scarce with the killers in the pickup truck, I ran Ophelia pretty hard for a fairly long time. I guess I got a little excited and overdid it a little, because she started running hot all the way from Brentwood to Spring Hill. I thought she was maybe just not used to being run as wide-open as I'd done with her and maybe all she needed was time to cool down, but that wasn't the case, because she ran hot all the way home and did the same thing this morning on the way in.

"I'm just going to tell you, Leonard. All this stuff with Teresa after all the years and being with her and having to avoid any problems with John—because he's still her husband, you know, and he's also my boss—and then getting embroiled with some jerk like Scotty Rawls over his wife, who, incidentally, I wouldn't touch with a seventy-five-foot cherry picker, I'll tell you, that's a lot. But it's nothing to me in the long run like it would be if something was to go really wrong with my car. All this other stuff is something that's here now and tomorrow it's probably gone, but none of it is eternal and forever like the Tiger is. Forty years it's been now, since I was a kid watching my dad trying to make it perfect--he died and it was totally mine from then on out. The Sunbeam was the only thing I owned back then that was different from everyone else and anything that was theirs, and it's all I've had for a long time that makes me remember who I was and how I used to be. That Tiger keeps me tethered to the better side of myself, Leonard. I hate to think how crappy life would be if I lost it."

. . . .

It was right after lunch when things began to get interesting.

Everybody returned to their stations to resume working on the day's projects, and that's when I saw Scotty walk by my stall and go into the main building. This was where Doris' desk was located along with the customer waiting area, and on past that was my uncle's office. I wondered if Scotty had decided to go and have a chat with Uncle John or if he'd been summoned. Either way, it sent warning bells going off inside me. I had the feeling something was going to happen very soon.

Sure enough, in a few minutes Sam came by on his way in to see Uncle John. He stopped long enough to point his thumb toward the main building and say, "Here goes nothing, Leonard," and then continued on his way toward the door. I watched him like I was one of the prisoners watching Montgomery Clift going to get electrocuted in "A Place in the Sun," like I ought to be peering out the bars and saying good luck to him for the last time.

Whatever was said didn't take long, and in twenty minutes Sam was back at my door on his way back to his stall to pick up his personal belongings.

"I've been dismissed for unacceptable moral behavior. I'm supposed to know better than to fool around with Scotty Rawls' wife. We'll talk about it later if you want."

"Why not now?" I asked.

I followed him to his work area, knowing all the time I was probably on camera and that Uncle John might be sitting in his office taking in my behavior on a monitor, but I didn't care much at the moment. I figured he probably knew by now that Sam and I hung out some together, whether he'd learned it by hearsay or if Teresa or Jennifer had mentioned it or if there'd been a private shamus on my tail for a while making a note of where I went and who I saw along the way, because if I was an employee of Wright's and just so happened to be John Wright's nephew then that gave him the right to do such a thing. It was a little much by then, I'll let you know. I didn't need any of it. It was the same way I didn't need my mother snooping around my room when I was gone or finding out what time I came in at night or if I was drinking and taking drugs again, I didn't need it, I was a big boy, and I certainly didn't need my rich high society perhaps-gangster uncle keeping tabs on me either. Maybe I was small fries in the world when it came down to it, but the secret was out now and the bottom line was I didn't have to answer to anyone, not family or business or even Jennifer with her warm body I sometimes felt compelled to hold against me when the world started making me ill. None of it mattered. It was to the point where I was finding myself a lot happier being without something than with it, people, money, sex, any of my many vices. I walked with Sam past the stalls with everyone inside them diligent in their work, looking up as we passed, and I knew I'd be happier if I didn't have to look at any of them anymore too. I was a ticking bomb and Sam was a flame, and being around him meant I was going to explode sometime soon, now, later, but assuredly the boom would someday happen. It was a sure thing that sparks were fixing to fly.

But I didn't care. I was more than happy to go up in smoke. I didn't want to be left behind all safe and secure with my paycheck and my childhood bedroom and Turner Classics on the nights when I couldn't stand life anymore. I wanted to be rid of all of it. I wanted to be free like Sam. I wanted to take my saved-up money and go buy myself my own two-seater. I wanted to hit the road and live life the same way Sam had, searching for something and anything and everything and who gave a damn if I ever really found any of it or not. I'd read Kerouac. I knew what to do.

"Don't go and do something stupid on account of me," Sam told me, like he was reading my mind. He was looking around making sure he had all his personal items before he left. I saw how he didn't pick up anything that wasn't his, like tools or service manuals or stuff like that, and I had to hand it to him for not being petty. I would have loaded up my pockets just for spite. "A job that pays like this is hard to come by, and you've also got the added bonus of being family. You don't do anything to piss your uncle off and you can probably hang around here forever. Hell, he might even leave the business to you when he gets ready to croak." Sam smiled a little at the thought. "I wouldn't count on it, though. People like your uncle have a bad habit of living forever. They're like vermin. They're not only like rats but they have nine lives too. I wrote him a check for what I owed him on Sunbeam parts and he never even blinked. Honesty means nothing to him."

"Screw him," I said. "It was never my idea to come to work here anyway. I just said yes to keep my dad happy. I thought maybe I'd reward him in his golden years by going to work every day and acting like I'd seen the light morally. I figured the more boring and vanilla I was, the happier he'd be. I think about how people got the chance to view him in his casket and think what a happy guy he'd been, how God had surely blessed him. If I think about that kind of crap too long I have to go find somewhere to barf."

"You better be careful, Leonard. You're beginning to sound a lot like me. That could get hazardous if you don't take precautions."

He looked around the stall and let it register in his mind what he had and what he was leaving behind. There was a TR-3 up on the rack and all sorts of cables and wires and parts were on the ground below it, gathered up inside an old hubcap. Somebody else was going to have to complete the job on the car, and I wondered if it was going to be me. I doubted it. It was too much for me and my tiny miniscule supply of experience. The TR-3 was a real classic. It was red, maybe the same year and model Dustin Hoffman drove Katherine Ross around in on their first date in The Graduate. Jennifer was a pretty girl, but she sure as hell was no Katherine Ross. And it was for damn sure my Civic wasn't anywhere near as cool as a TR-3. There was a difference I hadn't managed to bridge.

That was the way I was looking at things. Without Sam being around to listen to me wax poetic, life was going to get stale pretty doggone fast.

. . . .

About the only way I can describe going to work every day without Sam being there was if it was anything it was just plain creepy. I didn't go near Uncle John's office for the two weeks that followed, and he never came my way either. I won't go so far as to say we were avoiding each other, but there was certainly some kind of antisocial behavior going on. Being as unimportant as I was, I naturally assumed that I was the only one of us experiencing these feelings of sadness and hostility and an accrued sense of vengeance yet to come, because for the most part what I said and did and the space I occupied in the world didn't make a glimmer of importance to John Wright, who still had his company and his subsidiaries and his outside vested interests all simmering in the same pot. He had no reason whatsoever to worry about what his insignificant nephew might be thinking or what might be brewing in his soul. The way things appeared to me was I could harbor my hatred and low thoughts about my uncle forever so long as I kept my place in the workforce and didn't bring up the issue of Teresa and her relationship with my friend Sam, and whether I was loyal or not to the bloodline of the family or the company didn't matter; what mattered was for me not to rock the boat and to keep my nose out of his marital concerns. I think Uncle John would have been more than glad to see the fragile relationship I had with Jennifer end too, for then I would have no pipeline to Teresa's thinking and would have to gather any information on that subject from Sam, and plans were underway to dissolve that source too.   There had been more trouble for Sam, even after his banishment from the garage. The Tiger's windshield had been cracked by a brick one evening, and another time someone had cut the convertible top with a box cutter, making a dozen slashes to the point where there was no way it could be patched. Sam had to remove the top and drive around in a permanent convertible until his order for a new one came in the mail, using a tarpaulin to cover it at night to keep the rain and dew out. I helped him put the new top on when it arrived, an exhausting enterprise that took up the better part of a Saturday afternoon that left my fingers raw from pulling and stretching the roof and fitting it into the frame, and afterwards we sat on his front porch and watched a starling stop in mid-flight to land on the top and take a repulsive runny crap there.

"Damn," Sam said. "Sometimes you just can't cut a break from anybody."

He was still seeing Teresa, but their meetings were not so pleasant or fanciful anymore. Somehow the fact John knew of their trysts bothered her, and Sam was of the opinion she was growing fearful of what her husband might do if he felt so inclined to end their romance, Sam sharing the sad fact with me that Teresa had always liked money and found great solace in having it, and he didn't have the slightest cockeyed idea if she'd dare desert this money and its source just for the likes of him, he who had been good in bed once a few ages back but was now only a pale reminder of how those things once were. He knew he wasn't close to being capable of cozying up to her and making her cuddle his wares the way she had learned to nestle with her numerous bank accounts down through the years and her closets of clothes and the lavish recognition given to her by the high society of which she was a member.

Some of those uncertain feelings had filtered over to me too. I found it harder and harder to include Jennifer in my plans much anymore, only calling her from time to time when I was horny or selfishly wanted to hear myself talk. Like I say, the quest and the end results of it just wasn't worth the effort to me after a time, and the thought of my sexual indifference started to seem like a natural thing.

And so September approached and summer waned, and I became more and more inclined to leave work each day and go home to my bedroom with a Whopper and fries and sit in my bedroom with the air conditioner blowing and the television on. If I felt in a fancy merry mood I went downstairs and popped a bag of Orville Redenbacher, then climbed the stairs to my nest and watched whatever movies Fate wanted me to see until the wee hours of the morning. I went weeks at a time not calling Jennifer or communicating in any way, and after a while if I did break down and call she was non-receptive and at last one night told me she was seeing someone else. I didn't protest or argue with her on such a decision, just mainly changed the subject and asked about her aunt and Sam and how that was progressing these days, and Jennifer said she and Teresa didn't discuss it much anymore. I wondered if Sam had backed off or if it had been Teresa who had applied the brakes, and it occurred to me it might have been a mutual sort of romantic withdrawal. It could have been that the four of us were jointly playing out our parts in our own sophisticated starry-eyed bevy of scenes, and that this was the way real people in their own clothing and their private desires behaved in the world, that in the long run there wasn't any The End or closing credits. The lights went out and the plugs got pulled and everybody went their separate ways the same way they'd originally intended to do. Nobody had to break character at all, certainly not for some such foolishness as new or old love.

Eight

Just when I thought things were calming down and life was settling into an inconsequential passage of time once again, the news came out that Uncle John and Sam had run into each other at a restaurant one night and an altercation had occurred between them. Sam was eating dinner on an outside porch when my uncle spotted him from inside the restaurant's bar, and I guess what happened was my uncle, being among some of his business associates and full of whiskey and bravado, hadn't been able to restrain himself from walking outside and up to Sam's table and letting Sam know that even though he was gone from Wright's Foreign Automobile Repair he was still, in Uncle John's opinion, not far enough away from the state of Tennessee and especially Uncle John himself to be acceptable, and then made clear his particular point of view while suggesting it should shortly be Sam's too, else there were other avenues available to my uncle that he might choose to use to persuade Sam to see things his way. Sam had simply stood up, laid his money with the bill on the table, and then threw a punch that bounced off Uncle John's jaw and sent him backwards into the table of a couple having their dinner nearby. In moments there were members of the help staff who appeared and took hold of Sam and tried to bring things back to order, a process that ended with the police being called in and being told that, yes, my uncle was certainly going to press charges beginning with assault and ending with battery, so Sam was subsequently arrested and taken away in a city police car to be booked. The staff and John's friends all offered up their statements that the blow was unprovoked and stemmed from the bitter feelings of a recently terminated former employee.

Sam called to let me know what had happened and where he was presently incarcerated, and I immediately curtailed my viewing of How Green Was My Valley to hop in the Civic and drive to Williamson County to bail him out. I wasn't exactly rushed through the process when I got there, and had to sit in a vestibule and wait a goodly time while everything was being processed for Sam's release, and when he finally walked through a doorway I noticed he had a cut along his upper lip I'd not glimpsed before, and he told me with a sly smile that it was a memento of his evening with the shining lights of the local police.

I drove him back to the restaurant from where he'd been previously dispatched, and when we got to the Sunbeam one of the front tires had been slashed. This was not cool at all, and Sam said he didn't know who to give credit to for such an act, Scotty or my uncle. I told him maybe they were collaborating these days, and as the words escaped my mouth I thought how likely it was that Scotty might have been my uncle's pawn right from the beginning.

There weren't any tire shops open at that time of night, and since the spare was low on air we made the decision to leave the car and come back and get it the next morning. Sam was concerned about me missing work by helping him out, but I told him I was taking the day off tomorrow, that it was one of my sick days I'd been saving up. I didn't tell him that I'd not cleared it with anyone, my uncle or Doris or any of the mechanics in the shop who would be expected to pick up my slack for a day if it meant providing good customer service. I didn't care if somebody's car got worked on or not right then. I hadn't mentioned it to anybody, but I was close to quitting without giving notice. I don't generally act that way; I try to do my best to be considerate of others and always take the high road and leave a good impression, but something in the way things had gone down at the shop for the past few weeks gave me the inclination to screw the whole lot of them over before they did it to me. It was a strange feeling coming over me, an increasing aura of rebellion and hostility against my uncle and his company, but it was almost pleasurable in a sense. It was like I was becoming a young man once more. And I was going to war again, and this time I knew who the enemy was.

Since I wasn't going to work the next morning, I spent the night at Sam's place. We drank beer until midnight and talked, and all the while I had the feeling we were sitting there girding ourselves for potential trouble, sitting and waiting for an attack to ensue or a siege to begin, like there were foreign marauders outside the door wanting to do us harm and we had to be prepared for them every waking second.

"Well, they know where I live," Sam said. "I don't mean to sound paranoid but after what they've done already—Scotty and his pals or your uncle and his henchmen or the combination of them all—it wouldn't surprise me the least little bit for them to show up and start pitching rocks through the windows or banging on the door or some such crazy shit as that. It's like I've stepped back into another century or something here lately. This threatening and fighting and destruction of property is the kind of crap that went on forty or fifty years ago. I thought the human race had advanced a little further than that by now, but maybe I'm just doing my usual thing again. I'm acting like I have a measure of faith in frigging mankind. You'd think I'd have learned better by now." He shook his head. "The thing is, every time I think somebody or some group has gone as low as they can go, they always get down in the basement and start digging some more."

Not only did I not show up for work the next morning, I also never made any kind of effort to call and explain my absence, then compounded that by not showing up the next day either. I wasn't really sure if being absent two days in a row was going to qualify me for Employee of the Month or automatic dismissal, but I did know my going AWOL probably wouldn't go unnoticed. I wondered if someone was going to report me to Doris so she would let my uncle know I was causing a problem, or if any interest in my whereabouts or actions warranted any action at all. It could be nobody would notice I wasn't there or perhaps not see why me not being there could present a problem, or possibly the entire crew might be so apathetic about who came and who went that not a one of them felt like taking steps to bring the situation out into the light to be examined. Maybe I just wasn't that important.

. . . .

The next morning we drove across town into the bowels of East Nashville and found an independent tire shop that had a reputation for carrying off brands. Since the Tiger's size was smaller than most cars on the road, you couldn't just walk into one of the big franchises and expect to find what you were looking for. Anyway, Sam said, most of those places charge you about triple for something that's off-size just because they figure you're desperate and will pay anything to get what you want, but if you can you're better off going to a small owner. They'll not only give you a good price but they'll search and find what you need, not treat you like crap for coming in and rob you blind on top of that.

Inside of an hour we had a new tire to take back to the Sunbeam to change. Sam also asked the tire seller if he could get three more that day if need be and the seller said yes. This puzzled me, and on the way over to get the Sunbeam back on the road I asked him why he wanted three more.

"We left the Sunbeam overnight. Whoever slashed the first tire might have got tired of looking for me and come back and done the same thing to the other three. If so, I want to make sure I'm prepared."

The Tiger was still sitting where we'd left it with the front passenger's tire demolished, so Sam got to work jacking the car up and putting on the new tire. He had the entire process finished in about five minutes, and I was duly impressed at how professionally he had gone about the job. He could have easily been in a pit crew at Le Mans or Indy or somewhere, he was so fast and proficient, and I thought how it would have been if I was the person in his place doing the tire-changing, how I'd probably still be struggling trying to get the lug nuts loose, using a lug wrench if I'd had sense enough to have one that fit, which in my case I knew probably wouldn't have happened. If I had a Cadillac and it had a flat tire I'd look in the trunk and find a lug wrench that would only fit a Volkswagen Beetle. That was the story of my life so far, and I was pretty sure that part of it was never going to change.

Sam fired the Sunbeam up and told me he'd call me later, that right now he had to go somewhere and meet someone for lunch. I'm pretty dense, but I knew right away he meant Teresa, and so I knew that despite the fact he'd lost his job over his involvement with her it still hadn't stopped them from seeing each other. I wondered why he was so obsessed with Teresa, obsessed the same way he was about the Sunbeam, and although my step-aunt was one fine-looking woman and the Sunbeam was a great rare relic of a sports car, neither one seemed to be worth the hassle Sam took for having them in his life. It was much like the way I'd been coming to grips on my own relationship—or former relationship—with Jennifer, how I'd arrived at the conclusion that looks weren't everything a guy should look for in a woman, that it might be a good thing if the woman had some personality and a sense of humor, and that way when somebody threw out a pail of dirty dishwater from an overhead balcony and it landed on her head, and all the drippings and refuse slid down her face and removed her makeup and made a slimy mess of her appearance, then because it wasn't just looks with her it could be your stomach didn't turn so much at the sight, because even if she looked presently like God's worst piece of crap you still knew that beneath the smudge and the mess there was a good woman residing there, and you knew that with some soap and water you'd see her again and the mess would be gone along with the makeup, and it wouldn't be all looks anymore but something else more valuable, and you knew the feeling would last and nobody would have to worry about growing old and wrinkled and saying so long to everything good in their lives simply because it was all attached to how good all of it had once looked when they happened to be young.

That was when I knew in my mind that I wasn't going to call the shop and make up some lie about why I hadn't come in that morning, or why I didn't make it in the next morning either. I didn't much care about what the consequences of my actions were going to be. Maybe Uncle John would call to see what was going on, but probably he'd skip talking to me directly because he was such a busy man, and he would simply call my mother and let her take care of the problem. Well, the idea of that and how that was the kind of thing that could possibly happen pissed me off even more, since it seemed like my bad behavior wasn't anything worthy of being discussed with me but could be bypassed on to my sole remaining parent to decide what discipline to administer to help me see the error of my ways and change my course. I was tired of this stuff. I knew in my soul that I'd learned a few things lately and it was time to process them in my own manner, and it was nobody's business anymore what path I chose to take doing so. I could quit work and sleep under a bridge, I could throw away the affections of a woman with above average looks and find a rescue dog and sleep with it every night and never know what love and marriage was and that would be cool, or I could trade in my old life of cursing myself for every screwup I made and sentencing myself to a life of watching old movies and eating microwave popcorn most every night, until the time came when I broke loose and went out in the world and did something really stupid just to let myself know I was still alive. I'd been doing the same escapist shit for fifteen years now, and it was time to close the chapter, turn the page and move on to something else. Something different. I could marry a woman who looked like a Great Dane and then go out and rob a curb market and go to prison for a few years—at least that would be something new. It wouldn't be the same old, same old, me performing time-worn tricks that any damn fool could do blindfolded with their hands behind their back; it would at least be original--dumber than a box of rocks, but at least a brand-new act.

So, I took an unscheduled day off and then took another on top of it. On the second afternoon I drove down to the shop and went inside to find my uncle and tell him what was up to his face, but of course he wasn't there. I didn't want to leave a message with Doris, so I sat down in the customer lounge and had myself a cup of coffee and waited to see if he might come back. I left a couple of messages on his phone. When closing time came he still hadn't shown up, so I drove home wondering what I could have done any differently. I was pretty disgusted. It was like the story of my life to not even be able to quit a job in a normal way. I couldn't have a normal breakup with a girl or walk out on a job or excel at much of anything out in the world other than knowing what was on Turner Classics every night of the week so I could check out of my life and live in somebody else's screenplay for a while.

After a night of watching a Bogart doubleheader—Casablanca and The Treasure of the Sierra Madre—I steeled myself up and mustered enough motivation to go back to the shop on the third day and hand in my resignation. This time I was lucky. This time my uncle was in.

"I don't understand why you're doing this, Leonard," he said. "You've offered no reason at all for wanting to leave your position. I thought you were happy here. From what I've been told you were coming right along."

"I don't like some things that have happened lately." I surprised myself being so blunt and to the point, but what the hell. "I thought this whole business of Sam Thornton getting treated like shit by Scotty and you was pretty lowdown. I don't know how you're used to operating your business--I'm new at this, I'm a novice. But I don't like the way Sam took the short end of the stick. You didn't know for sure if he was seeing Scotty's wife or not. I happen to know he wasn't." I didn't say the first word about Teresa.

"Well, I know more about Sam Thornton than you think I do, Leonard. He's not the man you think he is. A lot of his references don't match. His background is different than what he first presented to me, and he had some things going on in his outside life that were averse to our company philosophy."

Uncle John sat there at his desk looking at me like he was on a high moral plane that somebody like me would never understand, like he was sorrowful that I would never know the truth of how the world goes around and the sun rises and sets.

"I'm not the dumbass you think I am, Uncle John. You might believe because I'm your brother's son that I'm lacking in the brains department and will go along with anything just like the rest of the family always has, but after a while I know what I see is what it is no matter if somebody keeps telling me it isn't. That's you. I don't believe you. I believe Sam. I know where he's coming from and I know you're not to be trusted. I can't do anything about it because it's none of my business and I don't run this place, but I for damn sure can't work for you anymore. I'd rather not have money than know what I have is coming from you. I'm twenty-eight. I don't want to waste the next twenty years of my life being around a rear end like you." I looked him in the eye.

"I know exactly what you did to Sam Thornton and why," I said.

Then I turned and walked out.

. . . .

I had what people would call an uncontrollable impulse when I got outside the building. I knew when customers left their cars off for maintenance appointments a lot of these superior assholes thought they were too damn good to have to go inside and leave their keys at the desk, so they'd just pull up to the shop entrance and leave their cars there with the keys in them and leave. These folks thought they were so entitled that each of the mechanics knew who they were and what car they drove and would make certain the car got into the proper area for its appointment.

I walked outside, and instead of going to my Civic I eased over to the waiting line and took a look at the selection to be serviced today. There was a Jag and a Rolls and two MGs and a really sweet Austin Healey 3000. I had the distinct feeling at least one of these gems had the keys inside them, and all I had to do was walk over and take a quick peek.

It was almost a clean sweep. The only one of the cars without keys in the ignition was the Rolls, which was the only one of the five I wouldn't have picked anyway.

It was a sunny and golden fall morning. It was a good day for a ride with the top down. I had four convertibles to choose from, and I opted for the Austin Healey.

I didn't hesitate or stop to think about it or anything. I simply walked over and got in, fired it up and backed out of the line, threw it into first and took off down the road. I wasn't planning on making this joyride into any kind of an extended journey. What I had in mind was maybe a five or ten-minute jaunt down Franklin Road, just long enough of a time for the Healey to come up missing and everybody down at Wright's to acquire an aneurism about where it had gone, how had it been pilfered, who stole it off the lot, and what were they going to tell the owner when he came back to get it. Heck, I knew they'd call the militia out to find it, so I didn't want to be the one caught behind the wheel when they did. I had just enough inside knowledge to know that there weren't any cameras on the side entrance to the garage area, but I wasn't dumb enough to think that nobody saw me leave or that no one was going to see a blue and white 1966 Austin Healey 3000 cruising around town and think nothing of it, that they'd just watch it go by like they would a Ford Pinto or my sorry faded blue Civic. People would notice it, all right, and they'd be apt to recall who was driving it and which way it went.

My plan was to drive the 3000 about a mile down the road and then park it in a lot somewhere, someplace where they'd find it pretty quick but everyone down at Wright's would still have a lot of acid reflux over it being taken, and as Ricky Ricardo always said, "some 'splaining to do." What I'd do was ditch it and then hike back for my own car, and drive away before anybody put two and two together.

But it was a beautiful car. It was a great car. That Austin Healey 3000 was the finest car I'd ever driven, and it seemed a real shame to give it up so soon.

So, instead of ditching it like I'd first thought and playing it safe, I chose to cruise on out the highway and feel the wind in my hair and listen to the throb of the motor. Whatever the reason had been for the Healey's owner to bring it into the shop, it certainly wasn't because there was something wrong with it mechanically— at least not in my book. I had never been behind the wheel of any- thing that ran so wonderful in my entire life.

I couldn't help myself. I had to go by Sam's place and show it to him. I wanted him to see that I wasn't a frightened little wimp who was afraid to take a chance and step out into the world at times. I wanted him to see that he hadn't been wasting his time imparting his philosophies and his knowledge my way, that I was more than capable of holding my own when it came to striking a blow for freedom from the oppressor when the occasion warranted. I thought maybe it would make him feel better when he knew there was someone out in the world besides himself that would not take an entire line of bullshit lying down, that he had brought along an- other brave soul to further the cause with him.

But Sam wasn't around when I got there, and since it was now going on an hour since I'd appropriated the Healey I thought it might be a good idea to get back and stick to my original plan. Sud- denly I was all paranoid and jumpy; I reckoned how any minute now the long arm of the law was going to appear and take me into custody. It would be hard to convince anyone that I had only borrowed the car for a little while to make a statement about what I thought was all wrong with this world I was being forced to dwell in.

I drove carefully back toward the shop, taking back roads as much as possible to avoid being seen, until I came to the parking lot of an Ace Hardware. I didn't much want to leave the keys in the ignition for some other thief to come across, so I walked into the store and looked around the paint section for a minute before dropping the keys on the floor for a clerk to find, then I pushed out the door and started hiking up the road back to my own car. I wondered if the State Troopers were going to pull up in front of me any second and throw me across the hood of their car, handcuff me and read me my rights before they took me back to headquarters to beat the living bejesus out of me.

I'd been watching too many movies.

I got about halfway back to the shop when I started freaking out thinking about how by now the coppers probably had my car surrounded on a stakeout. I made up a lie about how the reason my car was there was because I was across the street eating lunch, but I knew that when they checked my alibi they'd find out I was lying, and soon I'd break down during the interrogation and confess everything I'd done, grand auto theft, perjury, being the consort of another known felon. I'd be going up the river for quite a while, all for nothing, all because I took off in some rich dude's Austin Healey 3000 just to throw a monkey wrench in my uncle's operation.

I tried not to degrade myself as I walked back to the Ace Hardware and went inside to see if the keys were still on the floor in the paint department. They were. The Austin Healey was parked where I'd left it—it hadn't been stolen yet either. I started it up and drove back to the shop, knowing I was probably driving into a trap, but I knew I couldn't rest easy unless I followed through on what my idiotic brain was telling me.

I didn't see anybody around outside, so I pulled the Healey up to the receiving door where we'd started out from. I left the keys in the ignition and got out and walked back to my car, got in and drove away like a flash. I didn't squeal rubber or anything because it wasn't in the Civic to do such a thing, but it was still the fastest I'd ever driven it. I'd always taken it easy, afraid if I jerked it around or stomped the accelerator too much it would fall apart from the stress. But nobody ran out in front of me waving their arms or welding a gun to stop me. I got away. I looked in the mirror checking for squad cars with their lights blazing and sirens shrieking, but there was nothing there. It appeared I'd been successful with the whole affair, even if I knew I'd be turning it over endlessly in my head for some time. It was kind of sad, in a way. I'd started out making some spectacular show of protest over the way my uncle and his world operated, and I'd done it too, but in the end I hadn't had the moxie to totally carry out my statement. It was like the ways of the world had been dictated and set down as fact for so long that there didn't seem much of a way for me to change it, to make it shudder or shimmer. There was just too much of it to move.

All the way home I berated myself for a job not well done and told myself how I was going to regret this day later, all this being done in my head while my eyes darted up and down and behind and in front of me waiting to spot the authorities prepared to pull me over and carry me away to be James Earl Ray's cellmate. I couldn't remember if old James Earl was still alive or not, but I knew even if he was dead I'd still get placed with somebody totally undesirable when I wasn't doing time in the Hole.

I decided not to wait on my uncle to make the next move. When I got home, I called my mother to the kitchen table for a discussion and told her what I'd done, how I'd quit my job for no reason I could say and was going to look for something else very soon, and how in the meantime I was going to move out and room with one of my friends from the shop. I didn't tell her that friend was Sam who'd also just been terminated, or how he'd spent some time behind bars for dealing drugs, or that he was also, by the way, having an affair with Uncle John's wife while awaiting trial on assault and battery charges. There are simply a few things a fellow's mother doesn't need to know. Too much knowledge only causes heartburn and misunderstanding.

I went upstairs and packed my bag and loaded up the Civic with a few essentials. I'll be around, I told my mother. You don't have to worry. I'm all right. I didn't tell her that my main regret about moving out like this was I had to leave the cable service behind. I didn't know how I was going to function without the companionship of Turner Classics.

I drove to Sam's house but he still wasn't around. I was beginning to think he might have left for good already without even saying so long to me, but in a little while I spotted the Sunbeam nosing down the road at a slow gait, like he'd spotted a car in his driveway and wondered if this was another enemy attack. When he saw it was me, he pulled in and shut the car off. The top was down and he sat looking across at me, wondering, I suppose, what the hell I was doing sitting in his driveway when I ought to be at work. It was like a reversal in our roles, for this time it was me who had a tale to tell. Sam would have to hear about me telling my uncle to kiss off and about my excursion in the borrowed Austin Healey and how I'd explained to my mother I was a recalcitrant screwup and had to get out on my own and find myself for about the thousandth time, and then add in the fact that I was now officially homeless and needed somewhere to rest my weary head, which was spinning with angst and regret and bewilderment over what the future might possibly bring.

He listened with that slight smile of his on his face, making no comment or interrupting me while I laid out the gruesome details. It seemed the more I talked about my precarious situation the less dangerous it seemed, and soon I was finding a lot of it—actually, most of it—pretty dang funny and worthy at least of a good long snicker. Maybe living on the edge wasn't so bad after all. Maybe I'd finally found something in this world that appealed to me.

"You can sack out here for a while if you want," Sam said. "The only problem with that is I don't know how much longer I'm going to be around, and while I'm here I can't guarantee an angry mob doesn't show up or if the whole place might go up in smoke. It looks like to me your uncle isn't as cool with being in an open marriage as Teresa said he was. I'm beginning to think that you can't really take anything some of these wealthy folks say to the bank and expect to get your check cashed. They say one thing and it tends to always mean something else."

I unloaded my possessions and we went out to eat dinner and have a few dozen beers. This time we left the Sunbeam in the drive and took the Civic, since Sam said it might be kind of peaceful to be in a car that wasn't marked for death by my uncle or Scotty or any of their Gestapo buddies.

I couldn't help it. I asked about Teresa and how it was going with her. I hated being a snoop, but I sort of wanted to know if she was actually going to leave my uncle and run off with Sam, or if all this that had gone on between them had been nothing but recreational activity.

"It's funny how stuff works out sometimes," he said. He was leaning back in his chair watching a tableful of girls laugh and drink and get sizzled. It was someone's bachelorette party, and the eight girls were having the time of their lives. This getting married stuff was still on the agenda with them. There was none of the been there, done that philosophy in any of their smiles or laughter. I could see Sam look at them wistfully, like he knew he ought to go over and caution them all against the notion, to warn them not to grow up too soon. "You'd think people would get smarter just by studying history," he went on. "You'd think they'd see the mistakes their mothers or their big sisters made by jumping the gun and marrying some dude just because he had money or owned a business or inherited a couple of million when a relative died, but they never do. It's like everybody is bound and determined to do the same thing that was done before and is convinced that this time it will work out differently. It's as if nobody thinks the same bad shit can come along and happen to them that happened to everyone else. They're convinced they're the ones who are going to have a happy ending."

"It's something that gets engrained in you," I said. "I know I was the same way for a long time. As a matter of fact, I was that way up until a couple of months ago. I don't know if you knew this about me or not, but I was this dumb son of a bitch who believed that everything was going to get rosy for him one of these sweet days. I thought all I had to do was pay my dues and take a few hard knocks and everything would get better. All those dreams I had in my head would come true sooner or later, and I'd be through wondering about fulfilling my potential or meeting up with my dream girl and any of that other bullshit. I'd just blink my eyes one day and everything would be sunshine and lollipops."

"I used to think like that too." Sam drained his glass of beer and poured another from the pitcher. He and I always went to places that served beer by the pitcher. It was cheaper and we didn't have to wait so long for somebody to bring us another glass. We had the belief that it was always best to get tipsy in a hurry and not waste valuable time being sober.

"The thing is," he continued, "I stopped believing crap like that when I got my ass locked up. All it took was a couple of weeks behind bars for me to realize that it's the luck of the draw for a guy to be happy or not, that sometimes he's going to get fucked over and it's up to him if he's going to do anything to change his status or to just stay in the same position and get fucked again. That's the way I was thinking when I got out. I wanted to see if I could go back to where I was and this time land on top, or if that whole world of school and Teresa was simply bad news for me and I'd be better off looking for what I wanted somewhere else. But I had to be sure, Leonard. And now that I've seen it all up close I'm about ready to let it be and leave it behind, but now I've got Teresa on my fingertips, and I don't know whether to let her go or ask her to take off with me. What I do know is no matter how any of this works out in the end, I doubt there'll be any kind of a happy ending involved. I've seen too much and know too much from what's gone on in the past to ever fall for that kind of pipedream again."

. . . .

I remember that conversation with Sam, because that was about the last time we ever sat down and had a talk about serious stuff. I stayed at his place a few weeks, but I didn't see him too much after that, being busy as I was looking for a job and him always out hunting for something for himself too—not a job, I don't guess, he wasn't looking for anything that was going to keep him around Nashville—but he was searching for something that would settle things in his head and make it easier to move on. I don't think he especially wanted to leave town with his tail tucked between his legs, like Uncle John or Scotty or the two of them working in tandem had succeeded in running him off. I think he was too stubborn and proud for that. But even if he didn't possess those feelings of rebellion and bravado, there was still the matter of Teresa to attend to, Teresa Past and Teresa Present, and if any of that equated to coming up with the answer to the equation of Teresa Future in the end, so he was looking for the answer to that too. I don't believe Sam wanted to leave with anything still hanging in the air like some worrisome phantom that was going to follow him down the road the rest of his life haunting him and asking him why. He wanted a clean break of it, a settlement of the facts one way or another. He wanted to be able to live with the consequences.

He kept seeing Teresa and trying to make up his mind, maybe halfway hoping she would make it up for him.

. . . .

One afternoon my cell rang and it was Jennifer on the other end, which surprised me considering the last time we'd talked she'd informed me she was now with someone else and insinuated that I could start feeling sorry for myself at any time, since it was my big mistake and fault that she and I were no longer an item. She wanted to have lunch, she told me, because she had something to tell me. It wasn't anything I could do something about, but she thought I ought to know it anyway.

"Aunt Teresa has started telling me a lot of state secrets lately, and I'm pretty certain the time is drawing near where she and your uncle are going to split up. They've had this open marriage kind of agreement for a long time and seem to have been pretty comfortable living within their own rules, but it seems like since John got wind of Teresa and Sam all of that changed. Before, it didn't matter if he was seeing five new women a week as long as there were no repercussions on the other end. He didn't want to see or hear anything about what Aunt Teresa was doing, and as long as she kept everything under cover and beneath public inspection everything was fine. But the idea that she and an employee of his own company—somebody he had found and hired himself and set up in a major position—were playing footsies and didn't care who knew it, whether it was people of the community or in his political spectrum or any of the media outlets, well, that simply couldn't continue to go on. I think there was a huge flare-up and argument about how she needed to decide if she was going to be Mrs. John Wright with a foothold in society and the community or if she was going to keep going out with a mechanic employed by her husband, and no matter what their previous connection had been in the past, that was then and this is now. Well, I guess you know by now that my aunt is not a person who gets told what to do, and so she called John on it. Now things look like they're coming to an end. I'm telling you this because I think she's making a mistake. I don't think this Sam Thornton fellow is going to stay with her in the end. From what I've seen of him, I don't see it happening."

I don't know what Jennifer expected of me. Her speech surprised me somewhat, since it was more than I'd ever heard come out of her mouth at one time unless she was reading a teleprompter and selling a Land Rover on late-night TV, but I told her Sam wasn't ever going to do anything to harm Teresa or anyone else for that matter, and if Teresa felt the need to throw her exalted life under the train then that was her own business. I wouldn't worry about it too much, I told her. Teresa and my uncle seem to have a way of cushioning their falls and taking care of their own selves when it comes down to cases, so I wouldn't worry too much what either one of them decide to do.

I didn't tell Jennifer that in my mind I grouped her together with John and Teresa, whether she was a legitimate member of their social class or not. Jennifer was, after all, Teresa's niece. Her mother had been Teresa's big sister. She had some of Teresa's looks and had been on the receiving end of Teresa's money for some time, and she thought of herself in the same way Teresa thought of her own self, that she was inherently better and elevated and her privilege granted her the right to think of herself that way and carry it forward for the watching world to see.

"I'll let Sam know what's happening," I told her. "Maybe he'll think it better to let my uncle and Teresa work everything out on their own, to let it be their decision in the end. I'll tell him his presence might possibly not be required."

But I was fairly certain that Sam Thornton didn't need any advice from me.

. . . .

After a week or so I found a job at a Target in South Nashville, working in the Electronics department, where during my shifts I frequently had to go and check and see if certain televisions were in stock or when we might get a new shipment of cell phones in and if they'd be on sale or not, very important tasks like that. Most of the time I walked around or leaned on a counter and waited for somebody to come along who'd want me to unlock a case so they could look at the newest in video game software. I couldn't answer any of their questions if they had any, but I knew who to call if such a problem was to come up. All I had to do was pick up a red telephone and punch in the code for the P.A. to work, and then I'd call in one of the resident experts to come and take over.

I worked five nights a week until nine o'clock, so I really didn't have time to renew my relationship with Jennifer even if I wanted, which I didn't for reasons I've earlier explained, so that worked out fine. Sam hadn't mentioned any more about moving, so I didn't bring the subject up either, deducing in my mind that the longer I stayed away from any complications of life (Jennifer, my mother, Uncle John, Sam and Teresa) the better off everything would be, for the world, as everyone knows, turns and only stays the same for just a small amount of time, then evolves into something totally different that no one had an idea was coming or even existed. I was of the opinion that if I worked until nine five days a week and went to the movies the other two nights the time would come when the seasons would change and all the problems of the world would change with it. My mother would give up on me and pretend she never had a son to begin with, my uncle would decide to believe I'd never existed, Sam and Teresa would either elope or get murdered, and Jennifer would make another commercial selling a Cadillac that some rich guy would see and not only decide was the car for him but also that Jennifer would be the living doll who belonged in the front seat there beside him when he bought it. It all seemed like a plethora of silly life events to me, but it was other people of position and money and modicums of good common sense, and I had none of those things, so what the hell would I know about it?

I came home one night after work and Teresa's car was parked beside the Sunbeam in the driveway. Just the sight of it made me start to feel nervous, as if something drastic was waiting to happen under the expanse of the evening stars and I was going to be unlucky enough to witness it. At first I started not to go in; I told myself I could leave and go ride around for however many hours it might take for Teresa to leave, but with the way things had gone lately I thought it might be a better idea to go inside and face the music and learn firsthand what disasters were on the horizon. I didn't have much of an idea what progression they might give to their own affair's plot, but I was a part of it whether I wanted to be or not. I was my uncle's nephew, my late father's son, and I'd been the one along for the ride when this ill-fated unplanned romance came back into being again. My fingerprints were all over any evidence of what was to come one day, so I might as well know what the plot was so I could come up with an alibi to tell the world and show I really had no part in any of this, how I wasn't of the participants' world, how I did not hold the same beliefs as they did, how I was nothing but an innocent bystander.

Teresa was dressed in a royal blue dress and some pearls circling her neck when I came inside, a wardrobe triumph that made it look like she'd just dropped by for a moment before going off to be a spokeswoman for some elite charity affair. She looked like she ought to be on television, hosting a variety show or introducing somebody for an honorary award, and when she saw me she didn't bother to smile like she once had been required to when people were looking and I was some version of her nephew.

"Hi, Aunt Teresa," I said. It sounded stupid as hell to say it, which is why I did, and I tried to keep going on past her down the hall to where I slept, my pseudo-bedroom of the moment.

"Hello, Leonard. Strange to see you here. The last I heard from Jennifer you were still staying at your mother's."

"I moved out. She wasn't too happy with me when I quit the shop. She thought I'd let down Uncle John and besmirched the family name."

"Your uncle doesn't care. You ought to know that by now. He probably doesn't even know you've left yet."

"Oh, he knows all right. He was right there when I told him to his face. But you're right. I don't think he cared much one way or another."

"Frankly, I can't think of anything he does care about these days, other than money and his political friends and how many times he can get his name in the paper. He certainly doesn't care anything about being married to me, that's for sure. His only problem right now is that I might live after an ugly divorce and stick around town, and then everyone would know that I'd been the one who'd left him for somebody else. He'd be fine with it if it was the other way around, but he loses too much face this way to take it lying down. He's busy coming up with an alternate spin on why the two of us are breaking up."

She smiled at me sweetly, and I could see why men had trouble resisting her.

"Anyway, I don't know why I have to make you listen to it. It's not like I have to convince you that your uncle's a prick. You've experienced it up close and personal." She sighed and looked over at Sam, who'd been standing in the kitchen during this entire tirade, rummaging through the refrigerator in search of something he could concentrate on swallowing instead of listening to a repeat performance of all that was wrong with his ex-boss John Wright. "Are we still going out to dinner, or have you snacked enough over there that you're not hungry anymore?"

"I can still eat." Sam took a bite from a Kosher Dill and swirled it around in his mouth with his tongue. "Where have you got in mind?"

"Somewhere that serves alcohol. I'm in need of a few drinks to get me through the night. I want to be at my best when I see the lawyer in the morning."

I watched them leave and opened the refrigerator to see if Sam had left anything behind. So, Teresa was going to see a lawyer, tomorrow, it appeared. The ball was rolling now. This was probably why Uncle John hadn't been particularly upset at my departure when I told him. No wonder he didn't take much umbrage at what I'd had to say. He'd had other things to think about much more important than me.

. . . .

At some time during the evening, after Sam and Teresa arrived at a restaurant with a patio where they could eat a sandwich or a steak or fish and chips and sit beneath strung lights with fans blowing gentle breezes upon them while roadhouse music drifted out from concealed speakers in the rockery and the flowers, the two had dinner and Teresa drank gin fizzes, of which she sampled a goodly number until closing time came around, while Sam played it safe and drank iced tea.

They talked.

Oddly enough, it was not the next morning's meeting with Teresa's attorney that was at the forefront of the conversation, but rather the topic of who or what Sam Thornton cared the most about, Teresa, whom he had loved those thirty years ago for one magical night, or Ophelia, the Sunbeam Tiger, who had been his constant companion and friend both before and after his incarceration, who during that dark period sat loyally by and awaited his return from his journey to a world without light. At first the questioning had been of a teasing manner, brought up in a joking way, but as the night progressed and the gin fizzes grew too numerous to count the tone of the conversation took on a more serious and harder stance, and soon there were insinuations and accusations and anger on Teresa's part toward that mass of rusted faded metal that she implied was a sad mess now and had never been wonderful to begin with.

Sam took it for a while, and then suggested it was time to go back to his place to get her car and call it a night. But Teresa said she didn't want to go back to her car just now, she did not want to wrap up the evening's festivities just yet.

She ran ahead of him out to the Sunbeam and climbed in behind the wheel before he could stop her.

"I want to know what's so great about this damn car that it should captivate you so," she said. "Why don't you let me find out? Let me drive back and maybe I can see what's so wonderful about this goddamn thing."

"You've had too much to drink. You don't need to get behind the wheel. Something might happen."

"But you were going to drive me back to my car and let me drive myself home from there, so what's the difference, Sam? If I can drive then, I can drive now."

"I've never let anybody else drive this car," Sam said. "It's too dangerous. This car can get away from you before you know it."

"Well, I'm not moving until you give me the key, honey. We'll just sit here all night until you do."

It was late and Sam was tired. He wanted this night over with. More so, he told me later, he wanted all at once to be far away from Teresa, maybe for good, and if this was the only way to be rid of her, then so be it. He handed her the key.

She knew how to drive a four-speed. The Sunbeam hardly made a hiccup when she took off in first gear, only lurching forward a slight bit each time she shifted gears. Sam was surprised she hadn't gone into a ditch during one anxious moment when she gave the Tiger a little too much gas at the top of third. But she was doing okay. He almost thought he might even be able to relax until they got off the ramp at Lebanon Road, but then he'd have to slow her down. Still, he hoped they could transgress the mile to his place without anything too dire happening.

He was thinking all this until suddenly Teresa swerved off the road for no reason and clipped a Jeep Cherokee sitting in front of a house by a mailbox and two trash cans. The Jeep barely moved, but the trash cans went airborne and hit the street with a clatter, while the mailbox beside them uprooted and tumbled down the street several yards until it hit another car.

"Whoops," Teresa said. "Somebody's setting traps trying to kill us."

She managed to make it to the duplex somehow. She pulled up to a stop and smiled across at him in the dark.

"We made it, buddy," she said. "Now that wasn't so bad, was it?"

That was when the patrol car came up the street and pulled in behind them with its light flashing.

"Whoops," she said again.

Nine

The first thing the police did was run the tags on the Sunbeam to determine exactly who it belonged to and if it might be stolen, and although Sam passed the sobriety test conducted in his driveway (he hadn't been drinking) he was arrested anyway for allowing a drunken driver to get behind the wheel of his car. The funny thing was Teresa was given a seat in the back of the cruiser after failing her test, and she and the two cops sat there until the man in the gold Porsche arrived and she was given a ride home. A man who accompanied the driver of the Porsche drove Teresa's car away.

The entire time I stood on the front porch and tried to make sense of what was happening. I offered my advice on how Sam was not the guilty party and got told to go inside or perhaps go with him down to the station. I recognized the man in the gold Porsche from my previous episode with Jennifer, and I recalled how she too was offered a ride home and a free tow of her car and nothing much had come of it other than my neighbors receiving a check in the mail for damages and some dude coming out in a pickup truck the next day and installing a new mailbox free of charge. I'd held the opinion that lightning never strikes twice but decided perhaps this was not entirely true in this particular section of Denmark, where pretty entitled women never had to face the consequences of their actions.

I drove downtown and attempted to make bail for Sam again. The crew behind the booking desk was fast to take my money but slow to deliver on their end, so I had to wait until almost four in the morning before Sam appeared before me. He looked barely ruffled from the experience, still pristine in his sport coat with the patches on the sleeves and his hair immaculate and brushed. He looked as if he'd just got up from his seat in a movie house and was thinking about what he had witnessed on the screen, the plot, the script, the climax and the denouement, and was thoughtfully making his way out of the theatre to go home. He was non-plussed. It was like nothing that had happened earlier had been much of a surprise. It was as if what had transpired this night he had known was coming and in play for quite some time.

"Well, the hits just keep coming, don't they?" he said.

"Yeah, I'd think this station we're tuned to might choose something different every now and then and not keep playing the same old song over and over again."

"I think, Leonard, the fact of the matter is that once a guy gets himself firmly planted on the shitlist of the gods the fun never stops until he decides it's time to go take a King Kong plunge off the tallest building in town. Drop me off downtown and I'll take a survey over who's got the best rooftop for quick descent and if their doors might be open for an early freefall this morning."

"I don't hardly have the heart to tell you this, Sam, but they towed off the Sunbeam after they took you downtown. The wrecker guy said it was standard procedure in cases like yours involving driving while impaired. I told him you weren't impaired and it was sitting here safe in the driveway, but it was no go. He was insistent on how rules had to be followed and he had to do his job. I would have stopped him but he was bigger than me."

"I wonder why I'm not surprised."

On the way back I kept the radio off and my mouth shut in case Sam felt like talking. Most of the time he just sat and looked out the window and rubbed his jaw.

"At least nobody tried to clock me tonight. That's an improvement and a good sign. I don't think my teeth and jawbone could stand another round of beatings this soon. I'm also surprised the subject of my previous assault and battery charge didn't enter into the conversation at all. Maybe that's a sign that things are looking up."

The sun was rising when we got home. The tow-in lot wasn't open yet and Sam wasn't due in court until next week. Dead-tired, I hit the bed and passed out for a little, dreaming the entire time that all I had seen and everything I knew that I'd assumed was the whole and complete truth was really all fiction and somebody's idea for a bad movie, that what I'd just witnessed lately would never make it on the roster of Turner Classics in my lifetime.

That much I could be happy about.

. . . .

I didn't sleep long, because I wanted to give Sam a lift to the tow-in lot when they opened. I didn't know how much they were going to charge him to release the Tiger, but I had a little bit of dough saved up, and I was prepared to help him out if need be.

He didn't ask me for any of the three hundred bucks it took to liberate old Ophelia. I could tell he wasn't happy about the cost of such a fee when it didn't really have to happen, but what he really wasn't keen on was the amount of damage done to the car that we could see in the light of day. The side driver's mirror was dangling from its base and the headlight rim was missing. There were two long scratches down the passenger side of the door and a crease had formed on the hood from the trashcan that had bounced off it after being lifted up by the front bumper. Sam had already had to buy four new tires and replace a windshield and a convertible top, and there had to be a limit on how much money he could continue to spend on keeping the Tiger roadworthy. I could see in his eyes that it was beginning to be a losing battle, and I told him how sorry I was he was having such a string of bad luck.

"This is not exactly anything new," he said. "I hate to say it, but it's always been like this with Ophelia. Sometimes I think she's cursed, and since I'm the one who's always with her I end up sharing the curse with her." He shook his head. "I'm beginning to think one of us is going to have to wise up and put an end to our relationship soon, because it's pretty obvious we're not doing each other any good being together."

"I hope it doesn't come down to that," I said. "That would be sad if it happened."

"Yeah, but we'd probably both live through it. That would beat dying by a long shot."

"Maybe," I said. "But sometimes there are worse things than dying."

"You're telling me, brother," he said.

. . . .

Two days before Sam was to appear in court for his trial on being the owner of a vehicle involved in a DUI case, he found out that the charges against Teresa had been dismissed. It wasn't her who called him to let him know the good news, but Sam's own lawyer, who was about the cheapest council he could find to represent him, who told him that since there were no charges forthcoming for Teresa, then Sam as the owner of the involved vehicle was off the hook too. This should have been a happy occasion, Sam's not being charged as a repeat felon, but all he did was take the information quietly and said thanks. Send me your bill, he said, and hung up.

I've still got that assault and battery charge hanging over my head, he told me.

He stayed quiet about it the next few days. I could tell it bothered him that Teresa hadn't bothered to call and tell him what had gone on in the shadows of her upcoming trial, but it was easy to guess that good old Uncle John and his money were behind all this, because nothing could make a problem disappear better than a good splashing of money somewhere and some words of future back-scratching to seal the deal. It was as if the casting out of money and influence had been like a massive net thrown out by a mighty fishing schooner, and it had captured and brought Teresa back from the open sea to the deck of the boat, not to be used for food but to be placed back inside a safe container again, a large bowl where she could swim and look pretty to those who observed her but wouldn't be privy to swimming off in deep waters with some dark creature from a distant sea and finding herself in over her head and out of her safe aquarium. It was a marvel to me what a big dose of wealth could accomplish.

All this time the Sunbeam sat in the drive with its twisted mirror and its gashes and scratches and its busted headlight. I kept expecting Sam to be out there every time I drove up or looked out, but it was like he and Ophelia had foresworn their vows and had not the heart or courage to draw near to each other anymore. At first I put it down as a matter of Sam lacking the funds to fix whatever problems the car had, but after a time I sensed money had nothing to do with it. The wounds and the costs ran much deeper this time, worse than the sliced convertible top and the slashed tires of a month before, worse than the shattered windshield and the flaking paint and the creeping rust and the slipping clutch, the shocks and struts and differential problems that had begun so far back and long ago that Sam had never been able to stay on top of them, numerous realms of trouble that he never had the money or the time to repair; no, this time it was the heart and desire in him that was gone somewhere, and it seemed to me that if Ophelia had a voice she would agree they'd had great fun once, but now this was one of those things that like a bird had flown away and wouldn't return again no matter how many times it got called back, that love had wings, and there comes a time when it has to fly away. Neither of them would have ever believed it before, would have instead argued quite vehemently against it, but now the truth was seeping in like rain through an old roof. Their love affair, so grand and eternal as it had been, was winding down.

I didn't talk to him about it. I waited on Sam to come to me. I knew him well enough by then to know that when he came to a solution to the problem he would let me in on it.

In the meantime, just out of nowhere, the Sunbeam started talking to me. She wasn't Ophelia anymore; she had changed her name. She came to me at certain times those days and nights and whispered in my ear. I might be in the shower or stocking some new items in Electronics at Target or looking on my cell to see what movie Turner Classics was playing that night, and out of the blue she'd appear. I didn't ask her new name, but couldn't stop myself from listening to what she had to say.

She told me tales of how it was when she had first come off the assembly line and been shipped to America, how she had been purchased by a lawyer in Los Angeles, and how she had spent three years there before being traded in and sent to a lot in Albuquerque, sold there to a young man who made a racer of her, drove her at high speeds on tracks for trophies and money, and then she had been wrecked and sat for a while until a mechanic bought her and repaired her body and painted her a different color and gave her a new engine that never ran quite as fast as the original one had. After a time she sat inside old garages and barns and sheds for fifteen years, her tires dry-rotting, her battery dead, mice scampering around the interior and chewing on the wiring beneath the hood. She believed that she was going to die there. She thought that her life was over.

Then there was an online auction and a bidder claimed her. He gave her a new battery and fluids to give her life, then drove her fifteen hundred miles to Tennessee, sputtering and gasping all that long way, and for twenty years he gifted her with new things whenever he could, trying with all he had to restore her to her former self. Sometimes, she would remember, he would almost make it. Sometimes she would almost be the fine fast car she had once been. But on one of those occasions when they had been so close, the man had died and she had been forced to sit again. It was nobody's fault, but she felt abandoned once more. She had lost her lover. As so many times before, she wondered if this would be the end.

That was when Sam had come to her, Sam, her lover's son, who came to her and swore his love and told her he would do for her what no one had done before. And, oh, he had tried. He had done everything in his power, Leonard, even when he was young and had no resources. I shudder to think where I would be today, she said, if it hadn't been for Sam Thornton. He kept me on the road. He did all he could do all those years to make certain I remained special. When he had money, he spent it on me. He was always loyal. Faithful to the end. And now that we are the both of us at this sad finale of our time together he remains so. I know that he will never really leave me in his heart. I know he will never do me wrong.

But it is you I see now, Leonard. You are the next young man to care for me. There is a time for everyone and everything. I feel it in my instruments, in my chaise, and I can sense that you feel it too. Our time together is coming.

She spoke such words in my ear. I could not escape the sound of her voice, the notion of the touch of her, the sound of her engine that came to me nightly in dreams. I knew change was on the way and my life was fixing to take another turn. I didn't know how long we would ride together or if we could stay on the road, but I did know however long it might be it would be glorious. We would stay together for as long as the world would allow, and then, like Sam and her and all the others before him, we would have to part.

• • • •

On a Friday morning I woke at nine and went out to the kitchenette to drink a cup of coffee and eat a honeybun. Sam was sitting at the bar smoking a cigarette and drinking a cup already, and he pointed at the Mr. Coffee and told me to help myself.

"You got anywhere you need to be?" he asked. "If not, sit down. I need to talk to you about something."

There was an unfamiliar tone to his voice. It held none of its former caustic wit, its acknowledgement of how marvelously ridiculous the world sometimes can be, how fate can conspire to place a guy in preposterous positions that just can't help but be laughed at in the light of day and sometimes even in the dark of night.

"I've been searching inside myself for a few days, Leonard. I've gone missing in action. Perhaps you've noticed."

"I figured you'd had a load of crap hit you in the face and were just taking an eight count."

"No, if it that's all it was I would have already bounced back by now, but it goes a lot deeper than that. There comes a time, my friend, when you have to reconsider your position and do something to change your fate. I wouldn't necessarily call it a surrender, but there is such a thing as a strategic retreat."

He stubbed his cigarette out in an ashtray, lifted his cup and took a reflective sip. He flicked his Scripto lighter with a forefinger and watched it spin around like a roulette wheel.   "Round and round she goes," he smiled, "where she stops nobody knows."

I waited.

"The only reason I'm not gone from this town already," he said, "is like the fool that I am I've been waiting for some explanation to come down to me from Yahweh or somebody somewhere to let me know what this whole experience I've been living through the last few months has really been about. I thought at first when I ran across Teresa again it had to mean something cosmic, that it was of lasting and real significance for such a thing to happen after so much time had passed. I thought my finding her again was kismet and was some sort of makeup for losing her back when I got my ass busted for possession of drugs. I thought perhaps the time I served and the rambling and roaming around I did all those years after was a preamble to me stumbling on something true and lasting. Boy, when I'm wrong, buddy, I'm really wrong. None of this was anything close to what I was thinking it might be.

"See, all that time I'd managed to talk myself into believing I'd been in love with Teresa Payne back then, that it had been love at first sight and nothing that happened and came between us had ever really changed anything in the end. I spent thirty-plus years believing in something I talked myself into as a kid, and it took me all that time and all that effort before I finally realized I was dead wrong.

"See, after a couple of weeks of seeing Teresa, running around on the sly like we were in some cheesy novel, I knew there was nothing there for me. Teresa wasn't anything but another warm body to me, the same way she'd been all those years ago, but I'd had to make something big and grand out of it in my mind because I didn't want to believe I was just another guy wanting sex for a night and not some classic storybook hero whose entire life was wreathed in magic, because for all my years on the planet that's what I've always wanted to be. I wanted to have the best-looking woman and the biggest house and the best job and the fastest car. Today I'm looking at things differently. You get to be my age inching past the old double nickel in years someday and you'll understand why. There comes a time when you have to stop painting everything a pretty color and acknowledge where the truth lies. You don't have to like it, but you do have to accept the fact that it's out there, and one way or another you have to learn to live with the way things are.

"I found out today that the assault and battery charge against me has been dropped, that John wasn't going to press charges, which I guess is good and makes it easier, but the real reason I'm still around is I've been waiting to see if maybe Teresa actually did possess anything of what I had assigned to her over the years— honesty, inner beauty, kindness—but I've come to see she doesn't. I hate to come right out and say it, but she never did. I was wrong. What was in her for me to love I invented and put there myself. The Teresa I wanted to be in love with doesn't truly exist and never did. And it doesn't stop there. It leaks over to everything else too. There is no golden town where I'm going to be happy and content for the rest of my life. I can't tell you anymore what the one thing is that holds me to this earth and makes me want to go on living because I have no idea anymore. That's a horrible conclusion to come to when the sun's starting to go down on your life. And it's the same way with good old Ophelia. Forty years I've been driving that car around, fixing this and that, thinking some day the time was going to come when I could make her perfect and she was going to be worth a blue million dollars, but now I know it's not going to happen. It's not in the cards. Now I realize I don't want to try and do something that's not meant to be anymore. And so that's why I think you and I need to make an agreement right now, this minute, today. I think we should come to an understanding that might be the best thing for both of us."

I waited. I think I already knew what was coming.

"I think you and I ought to trade cars, Leonard. A straight-up trade, one car for the other and even Steven, no money involved. I'd like for you to have Ophelia and I don't care if I'm losing a lot of money in the deal. I think it's high time I let her go and for her to be yours now. I think that's about the only happy ending I can think of."

. . . .

At five that afternoon Sam had the Civic loaded and handed over the keys to the duplex.

"You've got the place for another ten days," he said. "I've already called and broken my lease with the landlord. She let me off the hook with no fee because she knows she can up the rent for the next guy that comes along. If I were you, I'd be looking for another place. You can do better than this."

He walked over to Ophelia and laid his hand on her hood. For a minute I thought he was going to say a prayer over their demise and the end of their love affair, but he didn't. He just gently patted her a few times and smiled.

"We had a heck of a ride, old girl," he told her. "You and I had a damn fine time."

Then he shook my hand and walked around to get in the Civic. I knew the Sunbeam was worth a lot of money even in its present shape and that Sam was getting the worst of the deal, but he'd been adamant about making the trade. I didn't have much money saved, but I wrote a check out for what I had and made him take it, even though I halfway believed he'd tear it up later and throw it away. That was the way he was. It still didn't look right, Sam getting in my sorry old car and leaving me and the Sunbeam behind for parts unknown, but I understood it. Sometimes there's nothing more you can do when you're standing still. Sometimes there's nothing you can do but move on.

But I was going to miss old Sam. I'd never had a friend like him before. I hoped he'd come back someday, maybe give me a call from time to time, but something in me knew it probably wouldn't happen. When a guy leaves something behind, he doesn't usually come back to see it again. Most times he's gone for good.

"When you see Teresa again," he said, "which you will sooner or later, tell her I said goodbye. Maybe she might be sad a little about me leaving—it's nice to think so—but I imagine she'll get over it pretty fast."

He started the ignition and the radio came on. The Beach Boys were singing "I Get Around."

"Ain't that the truth," he said. "Take it easy, Leonard."

• • • •

So, in a matter of a few hours I had myself a Sunbeam Tiger formerly named Ophelia, she from a lengthy intense relationship and me from a life that had always had trouble getting started. We were a strange couple, but who knew? Maybe in the end we might be a good match.

Not that I thought anything could be changed, but I couldn't keep from calling Jennifer up out of the blue one afternoon and asking her out to dinner. I made up some story about how I was fixing to leave town and that I'd like to see her again before I moved away, which was halfway a fib because I had no idea what I wanted to do with my life next, but I went ahead and made the date so I could pick her up in my fast car, my Sunbeam Tiger with the dents and the scratches and the rust, and maybe make her think differently of me after giving me up for dead before. I thought maybe I'd put the top down and hit the interstate on our way home from dinner and wind the Tiger out until the wind came whooshing in and the door panels rattled and the thought ran through Jennifer's pretty head how it could be we were fixing to go airborne and take flight or wrap around a guardrail as we were passing cars right and left like they were sitting still, and how she might think in a strange way I was someone exciting after all, and how maybe when this was all said and done it would be sad to see me go. Perhaps somewhere in her heart she might even wish I would stay.

She advertised expensive cars that cost a pretty penny, but she had never truly been in a fast car like the Tiger.

I don't know if any or even some of that went through her mind that night, but I do think she was at least looking at me through different eyes, so that was something. It beat the hell out of me going the rest of my life wondering if she even remembered my name.

"So, where exactly are you moving to?" she asked. It was almost like she was halfway interested in knowing my whereabouts in the days and nights to come.

"It depends. I have to find a job somewhere that I feel like going to every day. I'm tired of always having to be somewhere I don't want to be performing some task that the world would probably be a better place if I wasn't there doing it. It seems like as long as I can remember I've been selling things and cleaning up messes, and now I want something different to spend my time at for the next forty years or so until I croak. I'm going to take a shot at making myself happy for the long haul."

Jennifer was looking good as usual this night. She sat across from me in the passenger seat with the wind lilting her hair up and down her cheekbone. One minute she had that Veronica Lake look, then she was windswept like Grace Kelly in a convertible in Monaco with the breeze blowing her hair back from her face. I thought she looked like she belonged in the movies somewhere, not in anything new or modern so much, but maybe in something where she was Lana Turner's sister or Liz Taylor's best friend. Her hair was blonde, her eyes shone with the promise of being that special add-on a fellow might get if he took the plunge and bought one of those Land Rovers or Mercedes or Cadillacs she advertised on TV. However much I might have tried to sway her thoughts about me that night, she was still quick to tell me she was engaged to another now, as if to insinuate that I'd blown my chance before and now it was too late. It didn't bother me much, whether it was true or not. I decided to think of it as her way of getting the last word in, that she would be pleased if I pleaded with her to try to make her change her mind.

But I didn't.

"I did like you for a while," she finally admitted there at the end. "There was something about you I couldn't figure out, that I couldn't seem to get to, and I guess that intrigued me. You were the first guy who thought about things that I ever had anything to do with. I thought something was going to happen with us for a little while. I even told Aunt Teresa that very thing."

I started to punch the Sunbeam up to about eighty right then just to give her an extra added something to remember me by, but I didn't.

"You're nice, Leonard. You helped me out of trouble that night when I wrecked my car and you never acted like I owed you anything for it. Most guys don't act that way. I thought it meant you were protecting me because you were falling for me and didn't want to show your hand, but now I know that wasn't the truth. I think you're just a good person underneath it all, but you like to keep whatever's inside you all to yourself. I suppose that's just the way you are."

I didn't argue with her.

She didn't say much the rest of the way home. It was like she was thinking about something and she wasn't used to it. She was a pretty girl, all right, that was for certain. It was too bad I'd never learned to care what sort of dreams she had when she went to bed each night. It was too bad I'd never even thought about it that much.

. . . .

My mother, being a widow now, decided to retire after thirty-five years of selling books of stamps at the downtown post office, so I pretty much was compelled to attend her retirement party the USPS threw for her at the Hermitage Hotel over by the state capital. I wasn't there two minutes before I saw Uncle John and Teresa sitting at the center table with my mother, and since my mother had saved a seat beside her for me, I had no choice but to go over and join them. I didn't hardly know what to say to make the situation comfortable, so I decided silence was probably the best strategy. I saw Uncle John look my way and smile and knew he wasn't going to make a scene or have me bumped off at his own sister-in-law's retirement celebration, so maybe it wouldn't be so bad after all. I figured this was the time to grin and bear it and get it over with.

My mother was busy talking to one of her old co-workers, so Uncle John and I had the chance to exchange pleasantries.

"Hello there, Leonard. It's good to see you again. Maybe we can take a minute and clear the air a little from our last conversation."

"My attitude's the same since the last time we talked, so I don't know if there's anything more to say."

He shook his head, like he was dealing with somebody from another planet.

"You've got it all wrong, Leonard," he smiled, like he was a wise old elder or something. "You're paying no attention to reason. You've yet to allow me the opportunity to defend myself or let you in on the truth."

"You know what you did with Sam Thornton," I said. "I don't need to discuss it with you today or any other time."

He looked at me like I was a laboratory rat who'd swallowed too many drugs. I could tell he was all prepared to treat me the way he did everybody else on this earth who was lesser than him, benevolently but firm in explaining what was what, and I really didn't care to hear it. I started to get up and leave and keep the peace that way, but I thought of my mother and how this would upset her and decided to play it nice and do my best not to spoil everything.

"I did what I had to do to quell the situation with Sam Thornton and a person who'd been under my employ for a long time," He spoke in a low voice so my mother couldn't hone in on what we were talking about. "Sam knew the score, and he went ahead and broke all the rules of my company anyway. He knew better than to have relations with another man's wife, much less the wife of one of the people where he worked. It had all been explained to him from the beginning when he was hired. He knew what would happen if he crossed particular lines, and he chose to go ahead and do it anyway. He didn't care the first bit about Scotty's feelings or well-being. He just took what he wanted and didn't care who suffered for it."

I looked at Teresa, who was busy looking around the banquet room like she was counting the number of people in attendance, and I knew she had nothing to say about any of this.

"If you think I didn't feel bad about letting Sam go, Leonard, then you're wrong, because I did. He was one good mechanic when he wanted to be, but the problem was he was too interested in other things besides doing his job and making a good life for himself. I was sorry it turned out that way."

I was doing my best not to destroy the goodwill of my mother's retirement celebration, so I shut up and let it ride for this moment and probably forever. Whatever I voiced about Sam and Teresa and who was right and who was wrong wouldn't make a difference in the end anyway, not to my mother, not to anybody. After all, Uncle John and Teresa were doing my mother an honor showing up for this party and for being a part of the community and for donating their time and money to worthwhile choices. There was so much they invested in and did out of the goodness of their hearts. You could read about it in the papers or just about every night see the two of them smiling for the camera on television, at a celebration or an opening or attending a ball. It was like when they were around royalty was there with them, and someone like me was in no position to say anything to the contrary.

Because, really, who was I anyway? What did it matter what I believed inside my own heart?

I stayed and listened to the testimonials for my mother and ate my lunch like a good son. It seemed like the correct thing to do, for I knew no one cared to know what I thought about John Wright and his wife and what they did when the lights were out and no one was looking. I waited until dessert was served, mouthed down a brownie with some vanilla ice cream on top, then excused myself and slipped away.

· · · ·

The only thing I knew for certain anymore was that I wasn't going to move back in and live in my mother's house again. I packed up from Sam's duplex on the last day of his rental and stood in the driveway looking at the Sunbeam, which, for better or worse now, was my car from here on out. It was true its better days were behind it now and there was a question how long this new romance of ours was going to last, but it still retained its mystery and its class in my eyes, despite that lofty status taking place and precedent in years past. I suppose that is the way it is with a lot of things in life that were once held proud. Everything changes. Everything moves from the past and to a future where one day it isn't a part of the present anymore. Even after taking ownership for two weeks now, this somber knowledge still seemed foreign to me. It wasn't that the Tiger was such a knockout; the paint was faded and scars and creases and a fine line of rust was beginning to creep across the back quarter panels. She was looking her age, which bordered on ancient, like she was a mummy car that King Tut had once wheeled around the pyramids, the hot sun and the elements now winning their war with her physical presence, but I knew despite all the cosmetic beauty she was lacking I could still get inside and drive away so fast no one could catch me. I could still outrun them all despite the passage of time.

I spent three days and nights at my mother's before leaving for good on a Friday morning in early November. I was on my way east to a town called McMinnville on the Cumberland Plateau, about a hundred miles from Nashville. I'd been able to finagle a transfer to a Target there, one I imagined was the only one for miles around, located in probably the only retail spot in the city limits. Maybe the city of McMinnville wasn't quite as small as I imagined my dream location to be, but coming from Nashville it seemed like a classic hick town in my mind, which was fine, which was exactly what I was looking for, because I was done with Nashville and its bustling growing pains, its struggle to become another goddamn Atlanta.

I rented an apartment for six months, which was the time I thought I would need to get my records and transcripts and applications all in a row and have some peaceful time to think things through. I'd come up with a plan for my life at last. I was going to go back to school and get my MFA and become a writer of some kind. Maybe it was stupid and would never work, but I was going to do it. I was going to try. The only trick was finding some place inexpensive enough, since I was bound and determined I would be the one footing the bill. I was going to make my way on my own, without the aid of inheritances or rich uncles or having to resort to a life of crime to defray the expense. Maybe I was dreaming, but I knew I had to give it the old college try. There was a part of me that believed time was running short a little more each day. I'd seen too many moments go by in a hurry lately, too much of what I'd wanted to remain in place get swept off and blown away and gone from everything and leaving nothing behind but a memory. I was getting tired of imagining and remembering. I wanted to hold something real in my hand for a while.

On my last morning in Nashville, with the Sunbeam gassed up and the trunk loaded and the passenger seat filled with kitchen utensils and lamps and what was left of my record collection, I drove by my uncle's shop on the way out of town and looked at the cars parked in the lot and the ones lined up awaiting entrance to the service area. There was no shortage of eye-popping vehicles, bright colors and classic brands. I saw Jaguars and Mercedes and Alpha Romeos and anything else that was cool and classy a person could possibly think of, but I didn't see a Sunbeam in the mix anywhere, not a Tiger or an Alpine or a Talbot. James Bond and Maxwell Smart and Liz Taylor would have been disappointed, but I wasn't. All it meant was I was a lucky guy. I had something they didn't, something rare, at least for a while.

The Friday morning rush hour was over, and I could have stopped and had a late breakfast at the restaurant across the street. They had a good deal on meals there, breakfast and lunch and dinner, but I wasn't that hungry. I especially didn't want to run into any of my old cohorts from the shop. I didn't want to greet them or shake their hand or provide an answer for what had happened to old Sam when he left and did I know why he'd been let go. I was weary of thinking about it anymore, and I didn't want to give voice to how I felt about people with money who ran things and never had to worry about codes of behavior that had to be followed, voice my disapproval on how they were so uplifted in God's world that all they had to do was make up the rules as they went along and every little thing would be fine. I was beginning to learn that if you think too long about things you don't like—things you can't do anything about—then in the end it will be the death of you. Maybe it won't kill you in the physical sense, but it will erase something in you so you'd just as well be dead when it's through working on you.

And as I turned the key and the Tiger fired up with its special growl, I thought of Sam once again and how he'd spent most of his life sitting behind this same steering wheel I was holding, driving and chasing some portent from the past that might have once been his but had somehow kept slipping from his hands. I thought of those years that had escaped from his grasp because he'd been busy searching for something he had only glimpsed but had never been present long enough to hold. He'd thought Teresa Payne was a part of a promise, something akin to his Sunbeam Tiger, a form of dream he could have for his own that was above the dust and the blankness of the earth he and everyone else was a part of. What he didn't know was those conjured dreams were only false visions in the end. They were all in his head and not to last when the morning light arrived. Sam had believed the treasures he chased out in the world would come to him someday, in the frame of a fast car or in the touch of a beautiful woman. He thought there would come a time when those treasures would be gathered together for him to touch at last, all present there for his bidding, that wherever he went or whatever he touched afterward would join with the magical things he held in his heart, that such fine things would someday come to him. All he had to do was be patient and keep that abiding faith he'd always held and someday all the great treasures he had dreamed of for so long a time would be his at last.

I took off from the traffic light as if lightning and thunder were under the Sunbeam's hood. I headed toward the interstate to drive to my new city, and I knew my own dream was out there ready to begin. I had no idea how long it would last.

But I knew it would happen very soon, because I had a fast car to take me there.

The End

www.powderriverpublishing.com

Powder River Publishing

About the Author

Ralph Bland is the author of thirteen novels and three collections of short stories and novellas. He is a graduate of Belmont University in Nashville, Tennessee, and lives with his wife, dogs, his Frank Sinatra music collection, and an eccentric MG on the outskirts of Music City, USA.

www.ingramcontent.com/pod-product-compliance
Lightning Source LLC
Chambersburg PA
CBHW070512200726
48293CB00007B/2495